D0653152

AND THEN THERE WAS NO ONE

And Then There Was No One

GILBERT ADAIR

ff

faber and faber

First published in 2009
by Faber and Faber Limited
3 Queen Square London WC1N 3AU

Typeset by Faber and Faber Limited
Printed and bound in the UK by
CPI Mackays, Chatham ME5 8TD

All rights reserved
© Gilbert Adair, 2009

The right of Gilbert Adair to be identified as author
of this work has been asserted in accordance with Section 77
of the Copyright, Designs and Patents Act 1988

A CIP record for this book
is available from the British Library

ISBN 978–0–571–23881–1

2 4 6 8 10 9 7 5 3 1

To Agatha Christie,
the undisputed queen of crime fiction

'My only pyjama hat! You should have taken the other turn to the lunatic asylum.'

'If I have made mistake, the apologize is terrific. But if this is not the lunatic asylum what are you doing here, my esteemed friend?'

FRANK RICHARDS, *Billy Bunter's Double*

As I peered, stripped naked and traversed by opaline rays, into another, far deeper mirror, I saw the whole vista of my Russian books and was satisfied and even thrilled by what I saw: *Tamara*, my first novel (1925): a girl at sunrise in the mist of an orchard. A grandmaster betrayed in *Pawn Takes Queen*. *Plenilune*, a moonburst of verse. *Camera Lucida*, the spy's mocking eye among the meek blind. *The Red Top Hat* of decapitation in a country of total injustice. And my best in the series: young poet writes prose on a *Dare*.

VLADIMIR NABOKOV, *Look at the Harlequins!*

Note: Confronted with the eternally vexed question of footnotes versus endnotes, I have opted for the former. If footnotes resemble the subtitles of a foreign-language film, the repeated recourse to endnotes may be compared to obliging the spectator of that film to dash out of the auditorium every ten minutes to consult a bilingual phrase-book. Neither is entirely satisfactory, but I know which, as a reader, I prefer. G. A.

Prologue

Gustav Slavorigin (born July 4, 1955, died September 11, 2011) was murdered in the small Swiss town of Meiringen on the third day of its Sherlock Holmes Festival. That much is in the public domain. Nor, I imagine, will it come as news to my readers that it was in Meiringen's museum of Sherlockiana that his body was found by the festival's organisers, alarmed at his prolonged absence from a formal reception of which he was the guest of honour. As everybody also knows, he had an arrow through his heart.

Even before the peculiar circumstances of his death enhaloed his name with a morbid new aura, he had of course been the object of fierce speculation by Britain's and the world's media, and if there are readers out there discouraged by the prospect of having the sensational if stale details of 'the Slavorigin affair' rehearsed yet again my advice is to ignore this Prologue and proceed at once to page 23, where Chapter One awaits them. I am alive to the danger of redundancy. But I do feel that, if what I am about to relate is to be adequately contextualised, it will be necessary, at the risk of boring a reader or two, to narrate not only the private history but the public prehistory of those events which drew to their dreadful climax in the Bernese Oberland. Short as this *tour d'horizon* will be, I still wish to apologise in advance, as Pascal did in one of his letters, for not having taken the time to make it shorter.

Slavorigin was actually born in Sofia, capital of Communist Bulgaria. (An unfunny joke which none the less pursued him throughout his adult life was that, although he impressed strangers meeting him for the first time as being as quintessentially English as the Prince of Wales, he was in reality, ho ho, of 'Slav origin'.*) His banker father, however, was sufficiently well-off and, more to the point, sufficiently well-connected to emigrate out of that unhappy land if and when he pleased. Hence Gustav himself became a Londoner at the age of four and, except for his student years, remained one until his death. His gap year, incidentally, and much to the amusement of the braying upper-class lefties who comprised his set, he spent 'roughing it', I recall him quipping, as the pampered guest of family acquaintances in Amagansett, Long Island.

It was while he was still an undergraduate at Edinburgh University, where we were contemporaries, that he wrote and published his first novel, *Dark Jade*, a semi-autobiographical

* The 'g' of his surname, hard in Bulgarian, was eventually palatalised by the wear and tear of English usage.

account of a fiery homosexual relationship which instantly made his name and saw him chosen as one of *Granta*'s Twenty Best Novelists.* That was succeeded, three years later, by what I and most people have always regarded as his very best piece of fiction, *The Lady from Knokke-le-Zoute*, about a Belgian divorcee in her late thirties who, after being mugged in the forecourt of the railway station at Nice while on solitary vacation, despoiled of her passport, travellers cheques, credit cards and suitcase, rapidly subsides into first destitution then prostitution. In the hands of another writer, a short-order romancer whose brilliance depends upon his remaining ceaselessly aware of his own limitations, a Zweig or a Bunin, it would have constituted no more than a twenty-four-carat gem of a short story. What Slavorigin made of this slim yet promising premise was a multi-character fresco stretching to three hundred dense pages, a 'scathing indictment', as more than one hack reviewer was pleased to describe it, of the moral bankruptcy of globalised capitalism. It won him – and it would have provoked a scandal had it not – that year's Booker Prize.

There were to be four subsequent novels.† (He was not a

---

* It was dedicated to the Scottish (gay) poet Edwin Morgan, 'my spectral mentor'.

† Plus, published by *Granta*, an unrewarding and most cruelly selective autobiographical fragment, *A Biography of Myself* – composed, significantly, in the third person – and a theatrical squib, *Enter Godot*, staged at the 1993 Edinburgh Festival but never revived.

prolific writer and, the heir to one of Eastern Europe's greatest fortunes, he never had to be.) The first, *A Sensitive Dependence on Initial Causes*, the account of a deadpan young madman who, in the book's opening paragraph, scrawls 'Not to be. That is the answer.' on the back of an unpaid phone bill and, in its closing paragraph, swallows, one by one, a jumbo tube of barbiturates, disappointed all but his unconditional admirers by its absence of humour and its flirtation with the dated fad of magical realism: 'turgid' was a word that began to be applied to his style. The second, *The Boy with Highlights in His Hair*, a surprisingly soggy coming-of-age tale and more of a novella than a novel, passed almost unnoticed (although it was the only one of his works to be filmed – wholly unsuccessfully, I might add). But it was with the third that he enjoyed a spectacular return to critical favour, even if it sold considerably fewer copies in Britain and the United States than he was accustomed to. *Wayfarer*, a vertiginously synoptic six-hundred-page-long overview of his native country's twentieth-century history, traces the individual destinies, some of them interlinked, some not, of thirty-eight schoolchildren who posed in the nineteen-twenties for an end-of-term class photograph which its protagonist disinters exactly half-a-century later while searching through his papers for his own birth certificate in order to prove to the authorities, of whom he has fallen foul for a never specified reason, that he is one-hundred-percent Bulgarian. The novel's formal and stylistic maestria was undeniable, and Slavorigin was once more nominated for the Booker (he lost out to a Caribbean writer whose name the world has already forgotten), although I have to say that I personally tried twice to finish it and failed both times. (I doubt even God – who sees, and presumably also reads, everything – managed to get to the end.)

What followed was three years of silence. It was an all very relative silence, though, as he seemed to be seldom out of the newspapers, partying at Annabel's, holidaying in Elton John's Riviera villa with his newest boyfriend in tow (to his great credit, he never sought to conceal his homosexuality: the famous first sentence of *Dark Jade* was the brave and noble 'I have always pitied any man who wasn't gay'), firing off regular broadsides in the *Guardian* at the increasingly repressive policies of the Blair government. Then, when his peers were just beginning to forget that there had once been more to him than the playboy polemicist, there appeared – precisely, out of the blue – the book that was to transform his life and propel it to its premature and horrible end, *Out of a Clear Blue Sky*.

So much has been written about that book, even the most motivated of readers may well believe that this is one stepping-stone which can be leapt over. Yet I repeat: to comprehend what followed, and what follows in this memoir, we really must immerse ourselves twice in the same river.

The first surprise (of so many!) of *Out of a Clear Blue Sky* was that it wasn't a novel at all but a loosely organised collection of essays, rambling, discursive and more than somewhat repetitious. The next surprise, considering its title and, in retrospect, its unfortunate jacket illustration – the much-reproduced snapshot of the second hijacked aircraft, United Airlines Flight 175, about to smash into the World Trade Center like a motor-powered model plane remote-controlled by a mischief-making brat – was that only one essay in the book, the last, dealt directly with the September 11 atrocity. And the third, for which his hitherto hazy left-leaning politics had not prepared us, was the sheer ferocity of his anti-Americanism, not only George Bush's America but America *tout court*. 'Once a millennial dream of generosity, tolerance and energy,' he wrote, 'Whitman's rich and multifarious "continent of glories", rugged, rowdy, aphrodisiac, wild, elastic and irresistible, it has become a poisonous carnival of bottomless bathos populated by millions of nice, ordinary, gee-shucks freaks and crackpots.' Oddly, the one popular American artefact he owned to having a lingering fondness for was Coca-Cola, drinking three or four bottles of the stuff – *never* cans – every day of his life.

Since even I would find it tedious reiterating the book's contents in their entirety, I shall limit myself here to reminding the reader of a few of its polemical high spots.

The opening essay, on popular culture, was drolly headlined 'Say Goodnight, Gracie', the regular *envoi* of the old Burns and Allen TV show.* Slavorigin had always been a

---

* 'It is too often forgotten,' read another passage, 'that the cultural glory of the contemporary United States has always been its high, not its

passionate *cinéphile* and had, in his journalism, expressed admiration for the work of Welles, Kazan, Kubrick and kindred neo-baroque American filmmakers.* In 'Say Goodnight, Gracie', by contrast, he flayed the entire mainstream Hollywood cinema as it is currently constituted, a 'terminally infantilist' cinema whose products he likened to greasy Big Macs – 'and the so-called "indies" are Little Macs leavened with a few limp lettuce leaves'. Well, why not, that's fair comment, and there are probably many of us ready to meet him halfway. But consider this: 'If you have ever had the chance to watch those German films which were made during World War II by directors of real reputation – G. W. Pabst's *Paracelsus*, to take a single example – you will know how hard it is to pass judgment on their strictly cinematic qualities, less on account of the embodied element, restrained but pervasive,

---

populist, art.' And he singled out for praise the poets Stevens, Eliot, Pound, Frost, Marianne Moore, etc, and the novelists Hemingway, Faulkner, Salinger, Gaddis, etc, if less so the 'much-overrated' Fitzgerald.
* Even so, he regarded these as exceptions. The Hollywood movies which he truly adored, and which he dated meticulously as belonging to a three-decade Golden Age that stretched from 1929 to 1959, were almost all, so he tendentiously asserted, made by European immigrants, cultural and political refugees: i.e. Lubitsch, Lang, Hitchcock, Siodmak, Curtiz, Ulmer, Preminger, etc. And I recall how he enjoyed teasing his fellow film-buff students at Edinburgh with the (in fact, true) statement that he had never bothered to catch up with either *Godfather I* or *II*. 'The Mafia as Borgias, no thanks!' he would sneer. Or 'Why should I go see a film in which Marlon Brando hams it up as a big dumb thug with cottonwool in his cheeks?'

of propaganda than because we cannot help reminding ourselves that the actors who appear in them were themselves Nazis, or else Nazi fellow-travellers, or else moral morons prepared, for the sole furtherance of their careers, to collaborate with the unspeakable. So it is today with the contemporary American cinema. How is one to evaluate a new film when all one sees on the screen, leering obscenely into the auditorium, are the neo-Nazoid faces of Hollywood's current crop of performers, faces as putrid as faeces [oh, come on!], corroded by their very Americanness as an alcoholic's by a lifetime's intake of gin?' Or this, of one cultish director in particular, whom I dare not name, since Slavorigin himself, had he not later had more parlous tribulations to contend with, would without doubt have been hauled into court on a charge of defamation of character: 'X is an asshole and his movies resemble what oozes from assholes. They leave skid marks on the screen.'

The next essay, 'The Statistics of American Stupidity', was even more of a shocker. In it Slavorigin presented his readers with a childish if seductive proof that a statistical majority of Americans must indeed be as stupid as many non-Americans have always believed them to be.

'The first thing we should note,' he argued, 'is that in 2004 George Bush won his second Presidential election (against Senator John Kerry) by approximately 50.7% to 49.3% of all votes cast. Let us simplify these percentages by rounding them out to 50/50%, from which it follows, if we observe equally that only 60% of the eligible electorate cast a vote, that 30% of the country's adult population voted for Bush. If, then, we agree, as surely we do, that one definition of stupidity is satisfaction at the prospect of George Bush regaining the White House despite his uniquely calamitous first term of office, then we can already state without fear of contradiction that 30% of Americans are stupid. Now let us consider that 40% of the population which did not trouble to vote in the 2004 election and assume, for the sake of the argument, the likelihood of their being divided equally for and against Bush. Clearly, by the same token, the 20% of non-voters who *would* have voted for him are also stupid – as are, however, the other 20% who, notwithstanding the overwhelmingly damning evidence of that first term, were too dopey or too dozy to assist in driving the idiot of the global village out of office. 30% plus 20% plus 20% equals 70%. More Americans are stupid than not. QED.' (Is the percentage any the less among Brits? I seriously doubt it.)

In the third essay, 'Buddy, Can You Spare a Paradigm?', he developed this theme of American stupidity, along with 'its physically externalised symptom and symbol, ballooning American obesity', by linking it to what he termed the country's 'creeping mediaevalisation' in matters of religion and patriotism, two terms which, for so fundamentalist a national mindset, had become 'virtual synonyms'. Let me dip in at random: 'Were Rip Van Winkle to awaken today after a century of slumber, or even only a decade, he would be amazed to discover that the United States had meanwhile known an intellectual regression inversely commensurate with its technological progress.' And: 'For Americans the Star-Spangled Banner is not merely the national flag, it is the True Cross.' And: 'For the Bush administration the Geneva Conventions are just that, a set of conventions.' And: 'Yes, admittedly, they [the American people] are warm, friendly, polite, hospitable to strangers and kind to animals, none of which, alas, prevents most of them from being also just plain dumb.'

Since the next six essays were written in the same scatter-shot vein, the reader will appreciate my letting them pass without extended editorial comment. But to give you the gist of it: Slavorigin systematically excoriated the pernicious despotism of American foreign policy; the lawlessness of the political-military establishment, particularly in relation to its endeavours, by the illegal erasure of damning videotapes, to cover up the pet CIA technique of 'waterboarding' political prisoners; the sweeping aside of numberless international treaties; the ineradicable rottenness of the Republican majority in both the Senate and the House of Representatives as well as the equally ineradicable pusillanimity of the Democratic opposition; the kangaroo court of Guantánamo Bay and swinish hazing rituals of Abu Ghraib; the widespread wiretapping of telephones and interception of email messages; the neo-terroristic methodology of the entertainment industry ('in the America of the twenty-first century,' he wrote in one of the book's more reckless passages, 'pleasure has come to serve the same function as terror in Nazi Germany', before going on to describe Disneyland as 'that Belsen of fun'); the latent chauvinism of the nation's intellectual elite as reflected in the many book, play and film titles to which the adjective 'American' is appended as a talismanic all-purpose prefix (*American Gigolo*, *American Psycho*, Harold Bloom's 'classic' *Emerson and the Making of the American Mind* – 'Who the Christ cares! Explain Emerson to us, yes please, Bloom, but spare us your ponderous burblings on the American Mind, whatever that is'); the religion of business and the business of religion ('As P. T. Barnum might have said, there's one born-again every minute'); the ubiquity of lawyers and liars; and so much more besides.

Now, that done, let's zoom in on the gist of the gist, on the very last of the nine essays, the one which shares its title with the collection itself, 'Out of a Clear Blue Sky'.

It seems, by the way, that Slavorigin's two initial choices of title, for the essay, not the book as a whole, were 'Come, Friendly Planes', a paraphrase of Betjeman's still mildly infamous line of verse 'Come, friendly bombs, and fall on Slough', and 'Small Atrocity in New York – Not Many Dead', which aped the memorable winning entry in a *New Statesman* competition for the most boring newspaper headline imaginable.* Naturally, his publishers vetoed both gags

* The subject of the original had been a small earthquake in Chile.

as just too outrageous, although somebody somewhere nodded, for both still feature in the text itself. As he elsewhere writes, however, 'Let us have no excessive piety in the face of individual horror, for individual horror is the supreme constant of human history.'

The thesis of the essay is, in brief (and 'brief' is the word, since it is by far the shortest of the collection, a mere eight pages): notwithstanding the eschatological glamour of September 11 ('Ah, those images, how we gorged on them, how we feasted on them!'), notwithstanding the undoubted and, as Slavorigin concedes, understandable shock to the nation's system, a shock he compares not to that of the Pearl Harbor bombing, frequently referenced in this context, but to the sinking of the *Titanic* and the extinction of all the plush Edwardian complacencies which sank along with it, it was, from the loftiest of overviews – I repeat, this is Slavorigin speaking – a relatively minor atrocity, boasting (his word) fewer than three thousand victims and causing the destruction of a pair of skyscrapers of scant architectural distinction, leaving scores of others intact.

What followed was an abject and disastrously ill-judged 'poetic' description of the event itself, from which I decline to quote. Then a few, very few, words in memory of the victims, a gesture immediately subverted by a phrase I never thought to see in a text published by a reputable house (and for letting which pass, neither diluted nor deleted, some poor copy reader who had doubtless been terrified of crossing so touchy and temperamental an author, was sacked), 'But, after all, *they were only Americans.*'*

Slavorigin concluded thus: 'For what was, I repeat, a middling massacre, on the human and urban scale alike, when compared with the genocides of Rwanda and Darfur, the ethnic cleansing in Bosnia and East Timor, and the hundreds of thousands of deaths in occupied Iraq itself, to have been exploited by such excrement as Bush, Cheney, Rumsfeld, Rice and that pallid fall-guy Colin Powell, with the overt or tacit support of virtually the entire population of the United States, in order to justify the invasion of a secular country which could not conceivably have played a role in the jihadist attack on the World Trade Center – that was the true atrocity of September 11.'

It was, in short, a polemic deliberately designed to stir up controversy. Nor did the argument, indefatigably inflammatory as it was, possess any real analytical depth or sophistication. And, probably to Slavorigin's own disappointment, the furore he had so obviously sought quite failed to materialise in the British media. Aside from a rave review from a single diehard Slavoriginite, the book received mostly mixed and muted notices from the national press, the principal criticism being of the untethered bombast of its style. It did, however, become an instant bestseller, a rare distinction for such a ragbag of undisciplined musings, and the 'Out of a

---

* Emphasis mine. In the original the aside is rendered all the more provocative by the omission of italics.

Clear Blue Sky' essay itself was reprinted in the *London Review of Books*.

It was, instead, on the other side of the Atlantic that the scandal finally erupted.

Slavorigin's American publishers wouldn't even touch the book. It was available on Amazon, however, and soon circulated as freely as if it had been published. Naturally, in view of its author's reputation, it took no time for the first of what would turn into a cascade of newspaper articles to hit the stands. To begin with, and for the next several weeks, these articles did not much more than acknowledge its existence and the vague disquiet which had been occasioned by its British publication. Then there came a full-frontal assault from an influential neo-con monthly published out of Washington DC, followed by another, suspiciously similar piece in the *Wall Street Journal*. Then, as the rumpus gathered pace, and ordinary Joe Six-Packs were gradually made conscious of the blasphemous affront to that occurrence in their country's history which more than any other since Lincoln's assassination had been brushed by the sacred, even moderate rags began to editorialise on its implications for the special relationship between the USA and what Slavorigin scornfully referred to as the UKA. He was savaged by the tabloids. He was denounced, absurdly, as a Twin Towers 'denier'. Why, there was even talk of a diplomatic incident. The American ambassador in London dispatched a note to 10 Downing Street 'in protest at this unwarranted attack on the single most tragic event in the history of the United States by a writer who has been honored by the government of our nation's oldest and closest ally'. (This, as it happens, was slightly misleading, Slavorigin having rejected the OBE which had been offered him.) The response of Her Majesty's Government was that, while it too regretted the intemperance of the book in question, its author had committed no crime, none at least, save possibly that of libel, added a perfidious little parenthesis, for which he could be held to account in a British court of law, and his views, however offensive, were protected by the right of free speech, that same right, note well, which Slavorigin claimed had been irreversibly undermined by Blair and his yes-men.

It was at this stage of the crisis, just as the original press coverage was petering out for want of a replenishment of new developments, that, like a spider, the Web started to spin its own web. Virtual rumours ricocheted round the blogosphere before converging on an exceptionally eccentric website, albeit one which received many more hits than most such eccentric websites. It was called *For a Trans-World America* and the man who apparently masterminded it, even though his identity was nowhere disclosed on the page itself, was that Howard Hughes-y individual, down to the very initials of his name, Hermann Hunt V, notorious for never venturing out of his Scottish baronial-style castle in suburban Dallas.

HHV, as he was referred to by his mythologising cronies

and toadies, was by no means the self-made billionaire his trumped-up legend made him out to be. His grandfather, Hermann Hunt III, had founded the Hunt fortune in Texan oil in the fifties, a fortune that his father, whom it occurred to no one ever to call HHIV, had neither squandered nor augmented when he died of a ruptured aneurysm at the age of forty-three. While still in his twenties, HHV, coerced by family pressure to forgo youthful ambitions of becoming a writer – with, so word had it, Ayn Rand as his model – began the process of transforming what was still, relatively speaking, a mom-and-pop business into a vast tentacular corporation by diversifying, first, into real estate, then into the liquor business, then agricultural equipment, then timber and forestry, then by a natural extension, the proprietorship of a myriad of ultra-reactionary publications.* It was whispered meanwhile that an indeterminate number of shady organisations, all of them based in the West and South-West of the country's hinterland, that 'mainland of madness', as Slavorigin had dubbed it, owed their inexplicable solvency to his generous financial backing.

Spoken of in this context were several survivalist communes in the Anaconda Mountains of Montana. A white supremacist group which held covert recruiting sessions in a desert motel, the Clandestine Inn, located seventy miles or so

---

* Trees and newspapers, after all, form two successive generations of the same dynasty, the latter being the literate offspring of the bluff, inarticulate former, like college-educated children of peasant stock.

from Reno, Nevada, and owned by a former Grand Wizard of the Klu Klux Klan. The Neo-McCarthy Brotherhood, anti-Jewish, anti-black, anti-Muslim, anti-Catholic, anti-French and, although one assumes just for old times' sake, anti-Communist. The Knights of the White Camelia, a fraternity of Doomsday prophesiers whose mailing address was a shopping mall in Eugene, Oregon, and all of whose members, running their respective businesses on a pleasantly profitable day-by-day footing while in anticipation of the looming Rapture, belonged to divers Rotary Clubs and Chambers of Commerce. These and many, many others had benefited from HHV's inexhaustible munificence.

Then, suddenly, the website began twitching with a whole new set of instructions to the faithful. Nothing connected with HHV, however, was ever straightforward. If you sought to decipher them, you had to print out each of the site's four pages, cut them up into two unequal halves, unequal in one and only one fashion (i.e. one fat oblong and one thin one, each oblong being parallel to one of the four sides of the rectangular page itself, and no two widths being identical), then paste them together again, but differently, like the four individually incomplete and independently meaningless segments of a pirate's treasure chart. Once they had been successfully recombined, and it had all fallen into place, the very first change to catch the eye was an unexpected refinement of the site's typeface, causing its name now to read *For a Trans-World America*. What was the point, you asked yourself for a moment, of those five ugly bold-type caps? But only for a moment. A moment later enlightenment irradiated the screen. F.A.T.W.A.

The acronym was patently intended to remind impressionable bloggers of the Salman Rushdie affair, an affair which, for most of us, seems already to belong to a dim, nearly unknowable past when (in a narrative that Chesterton would not have repudiated) a significant fraction of the planet's population had actually set off, by plane or by proxy, in pursuit of a single hapless human being. In a world in which terrorism itself has become globalised, we are all potential Salman Rushdies now, are we not, so who could be the object of this new personalised fatwa?

It was of course Slavorigin – Slavorigin who had blasphemed against the American creed, who had lampooned its prophets ('the so-called, pompously so-called, Founding Fathers whose fabled Constitution is about as relevant to the contemporary world as the Ten Commandments') and spat upon its martyrs (the fallen of September 11).

If the website's cunning dynamics still made it impossible to know for sure who was calling the shots, even a technological duffer, blessed with a modicum of patience and luck, would have been able to work out what was at stake. All it required of the committed hacker was a diligent bout of clicking, copying and pasting. Then, assuming a few boobytraps had been sidestepped, the screen would display a cute little rebus whose pictorial clues, including a popular coconut-filled chocolate bar (simple), the forementioned town of Eugene, Oregon (even simpler) and a movie by the director Sam Peckinpah (a bit trickier), would, when aligned in the correct order, end by generating the unequivocal message: 'A bounty of one hundred million dollars for the head of Gustav Slavorigin'.

One hundred million dollars! That put those stingy mad mullahs in their place. And yes, before long, through deepest cyberspace coursed the Chinese whisper that scores of claimants – at least one of them said, with a tremor of excitement, to be a woman – were boarding trains and planes, were heading for London, had already landed at Heathrow, on the first stage of the million-dollar crusade.

What happened next everybody knows. Like Rushdie before him, Slavorigin instantly went into hiding. Withdrawing from circulation, from the social and literary circus of which he had been both cynosure and clown, he found himself escorted, in the weeks that followed, weeks that would drag into months, and months into years, from one safe house to another.

During his long internal exile he was, however, neither idle nor suicidal. The despair he must initially have experienced – the more so as, to nobody's surprise, the American government, taking its lead from the British, refused to intervene – began to be cushioned, after a rigorously cloistered first year, by an occasional dinner in town, at the Caprice or the Ivy, by a starry gala première at Covent

Garden, the sole sign of his unannounced attendance being the proximity of two hefty minders wearing wraparound dark glasses night and day, pacing up and down outside restaurant or theatre rain and shine.

Then, almost exactly two years into his ordeal, he completed another book, a shortish thriller (of sorts, naturally).

How to describe *A Reliable Narrator*? Its opening chapter resembles the concluding chapter of a whodunit, one that just happens never actually to have been written. Thus the reader of Slavorigin's book (I mean, the book which *was* written) cannot hope to comprehend the picturesque twists of this first-chapter denouement since, of the murder which has clearly taken place, the only detail to which he is made privy is the identity of the murderer, a murderer who has already been apprehended, charged, tried, found guilty and sentenced to life imprisonment. Or, rather, an *alleged* murderer. For, as the reader comes to realise, there has occurred a gross miscarriage of justice. The real murderer (*A Reliable Narrator* is written in the first person, as if we were inside this murderer's head) has eluded the law, has, as they say, got away with it. But therein lies his dilemma. It transpires that the murder he committed was no more than a parenthesis, open then closed again, in an otherwise suffocatingly dingy existence. The protagonist was a nonentity before he committed it and, never having had the chance to bask in the limelight of guilt, never having enjoyed his fifteen minutes of infamy, he has become a nonentity all over again.

Just imagine the agony of his frustration. To have destroyed a fellow creature, to have barehandedly squeezed the last breath out of 'a whorehouse miscarriage, a lying, foul-mouthed, poo-flinging ape', yet to gaze into his shaving mirror every morning and see gazing back at him the same old pre-murder loser – this becomes so insufferable to his self-esteem that he howls out his guilt to anybody who will listen to him. But nobody will. Nobody but the reader, of course, who alone *knows*.

Hence the title. That first-person protagonist is no canonic unreliable narrator, such a tired old cliché of postmodernism now, but a perfectly reliable narrator, except that not a single soul is prepared to rely on him.

A Reliable Narrator was published to a set of reviews, not only in Britain, that most writers would die for. Which is undoubtedly why its author was invited to Meiringen by the organisers of its first Sherlock Holmes Festival. (Why he agreed to go is another question.) And which is also when my own part in his story begins.

COUNTY LIBRARY
H855310
ROSCOMMON
F

Chapter One

It was while commuting homeward on the 11.03 from Moreton-in-Marsh to London Paddington one foggy Monday forenoon in early September that I received on my mobile phone the call that was to change everything. Since the previous December I had been renting a pretty weekend cottage in the Gloucestershire village of Blockley. The cottage, Waterside by name, sat sandwiched between my landlady's grand house and a lively though apparently unlived-in little stream that could be depended on, in anything approaching a downpour, to overflow its timid banks. I would journey down to Moreton on Friday afternoons – on, by what was for me a delightful windfall of a coincidence, the 4.50 from Paddington (yes, really) – then make the same trip in reverse three days later. My train, in both directions, was invariably late, but seldom long enough to put me to serious inconvenience.*

* Ever since Mussolini got the trains running on time the British have behaved as though there were something inherently Fascistic about a competently managed railway network.

So there I was, snugly settled in a first-class compartment, reading, with a view to writing an eventual review for the *Spectator*, a fat, virtuosically executed novel by one of that new breed of American *wunderkinder* who, I would be lying if I denied it, are positively bloated with talent but who are also just too fucking pleased with themselves – its title, *The Theory of Colonic Irrigation*, should tell you all you need to know about the sort of thing it was. Since I was already aware that this was a book destined to be jettisoned as soon as my review had been delivered, I was in the process of pencilling some cramped, crabbed notes in the margins of its own pages when, at the Oxford stop, a single, rather extraordinary passenger boarded my nearly empty compartment. He stood for a minute in the doorway as though searching for a friendly or just a familiar face, then for a reason known only to himself sat down in the seat directly opposite mine.

As long as we tarried in Oxford, I felt an obscure compulsion to keep both my eyes trained on the text in front of me and even forebore, for the duration, from dabbing at my smarting nose – I was on the mend from a protracted head cold – with the third of four paper napkins which I had filched for that purpose from the buffet-bar where I had earlier bought a cup of muddy coffee. (The first two snot-saturated napkins were stuffed away in the clammy depths of my jacket pocket.) At long last the train started to glide out of the station, a plummy Indian voice on the loudspeaker alerted the latest intake of passengers to the sandwiches, pastries and light refreshments available to them, and even if I don't recall having had the sensation, one I am especially prone to, of being spied upon by some unseen observer, I could no longer resist peeking at my fellow-traveller over the top of the novel, as thick and doughy as a wholemeal loaf, that I held in my hands.

I *was* being spied upon. The man who had sat down opposite me had, I noted uneasily, a livid complexion, a shock of white hair, an unalluring black patch over his left eye which lent him the corny charisma of the Demon King in a provincial pantomime and an unpatched right eye which was staring straight at me. No milquetoast in an awkward situation, I immediately proceeded to stare back, to the point of insolence. As I did, I found myself qualifying my crude first impression. Swimming into sharper focus, he turned out to be less fleshily flamboyant than the description above must have made him sound. His complexion was of the wind-and-weatherbeaten type the English refer to as 'ruddy', his hair, if untidy enough, had nevertheless submitted to the recent attentions of a comb, his eyepatch was just an eyepatch. As he was also wearing a rough, fibrous three-piece suit with outsized trouser turn-ups and complicatedly laced-up hiking-boots, I had him pegged for some maverick Oxford classics don, although whether he was loved or feared by his, I guessed, handful of students was beyond my powers of impromptu on-the-spot speculation.

None of which alters the fact that he was still staring at me. He had no reading matter of his own, none visible on his person, at any rate, no scuffed leather briefcase containing papers with which he might have whiled away the trip by consulting or marking. He had nothing to do, in short, but stare at me. Which he went on doing until it was no longer funny. Did he recognise me? Unlikely. One advantage, I thought grimly, of being only a semi-wellknown writer is that you can travel incognito on public transport. No, not grimly. No hackneyed adverbs, please. I thought, I just thought. Did he confuse me with David Hockney, to whom I bear a superficial resemblance (blond hair, prominent horn-rimmed glasses)? Since I knew I wasn't going to be able to keep up for very much longer our ping-pong game of stare and counterstare, something would soon have to give.

Suddenly, inside the same jacket pocket into which I had stuffed the soaking napkin balls, my mobile, which I had forgotten to switch off, started ringing, loud enough to cause us both momentarily to lose our stride in the game. Now he no longer stared, he glared at me, more unnervingly than if he had been in possession of both his eyes. (In the land of the seeing, the one-eyed man is somehow still king.) It was all the more awkward in that our compartment had been designated the train's sole Quiet Coach, one in which the use of mobiles was banned – which is precisely why I chose it – and my telephone's ring-tone was Tchaikovsky's Walt-Disneyan 'Waltz of the Flowers'.

Under his glowering gaze, I retrieved the elegant, hateful, indispensable little object from my pocket, flipped open its lid and put it to my ear.

'Hello?' I whispered.

It was my literary agent, Carole Blake – Carole who, after all, could be said to work for me, who retained fifteen per-cent of my royalties, yet by whom I was still, so many years since I joined the agency, ever so slightly intimidated.

'Ah, Carole,' I said. 'Listen, can I ring you when I get home? I'm on a train and I'm not really supposed to be making phone calls. Or taking them.'

But the call wasn't one that could be postponed. The very next day she was flying to New York on agenting business and needed an immediate yes-or-no reponse.

What she had to tell me was this. To commemorate the twentieth anniversary of its Sherlock Holmes Museum, whose doors were first opened to the public in 1991, the Swiss town of Meiringen, in the heart of the Bernese Ober-land, its main claim on the attention of the tourist industry being the proximity of the Reichenbach Falls,* had organised a Sherlock Holmes Festival to which erudite Sherlockians had been invited from all over the world. Since my own most recent work of fiction was *The Unpublished Case-Book of*

---

* Over which Sir Arthur Conan Doyle, desirous of ridding himself once and for all of what had become a beaky, brilliant albatross around his neck, chose to have Holmes, in the story titled 'The Final Problem', plunge to his death in the grip of his arch-enemy Professor Moriarty.

Sherlock Holmes, and since my German publisher, Martin Hielscher,* had realised at the eleventh hour that my presence at such an event might be crucial to the book's successful launch, she asked if I would be willing to fly to Switzerland three days hence, all arrangements made and all expenses paid.

Ordinarily I would have at once refused. Not only have I come to loathe travelling to Europe and further afield, from a fear less of flying than of airports, but I flee all fairs, festivals and literary dos. Even under the sole pressure of Carole's steely entreaties, I would at least have hemmed and hawed before no doubt eventually caving in. Yet now I had Cyclops to contend with, along with my head cold.

'Oh, Carole, I don't know,' I whispered back, holding the mobile in my left hand and cupping the right over my mouth as though I were about to sneeze. 'I mean, I'll do my little forty-five-minute stint and then what? It feels like so much hassle for so little result. Besides, as you can probably hear, I'm just getting over a bad cold.'

'Gilbert,' said Carole, who enjoyed the advantage over me of not being obliged to lower her voice, 'I do think that if Martin – Martin, who has really got behind you – believes your attendance will prove a boost to sales, you yourself could unselfishly put up with a little hassle.'

There then came the knockdown argument to which no writer has ever been capable of responding.

---

* Of the Munich-based house Beck.

'Or don't you want your books to sell?'

Without speaking, meanwhile, the Demon King gave the vibrating window between us three impatient taps with the colossally thick, hairy knuckles of his right hand, drawing my attention to the words 'Quiet Coach' stencilled on its pane.

I frantically nodded at him, asked Carole if I might have an hour or two to think it over, was told not, then at last helplessly agreed.

'Oh, very well. Tell them to go ahead and make the arrangements.'

Adding a barely audible 'Bye', I snapped the mobile shut, made a silently apologetic gesture to my still unappeased *vis-à-vis* (who was to vanish from my life, as equally from this memoir of it, the instant we arrived at Paddington, leaving as little trace of his intervention in either as a burst soap bubble), and slouched down behind *The Theory of Colonic Irrigation* while the train tranquilly unzipped the country's flies from Oxford to London.

Chapter Two

Back in my Notting Hill *pied-à-terre*, I checked my email, not a convenience of the cottage in Blockley, and found that I had been preceded by two separate communications from Meiringen.

The first of these was in the way of a round-robin flyer for the Festival, which had hopes of becoming, I learned, a regular and even annual event. The second specifically targeted me. I was thanked for 'gracing our festival with your august self' and afforded the information I needed regarding the airline company I was to fly with, the reference number of my e-ticket, by whom I would be met at Zurich airport, and the like. Also what was expected of me personally. There would be a presentation by my translator Jochen Schimmang, himself a prizewinning novelist and by now a dear friend of mine, followed by a reading by me of one of the tales from my collection. (Knowing what was coming, I had already, on the train, mentally selected the shortest of them, 'The Giant Rat of Sumatra', alluded to by Holmes in 'The Sussex Vampire' as 'a story for which the world is not yet prepared'.) The evening would end with a public Q & A session, one that risked being 'stormy', I was gleefully warned, in view of the high quota of Holmes fanatics expected to attend and, for many of them, the near-sacreligious liberties taken by my book.

I printed out both emails, slipped into my suitcase the one I'd be required to show at Heathrow and took the other off to study over a coffee in a Catalan delicatessen I frequented, the Salvador Deli, across the street from me in Portobello Road.

It was three pages long. Down the left-hand side of its first page zigzagged a *faux*-slapdash formation of four picture-postcard views of Meiringen: a chalet decked with multicoloured pennants; cows grazing on a gently tilting meadow; a bluish-white Alplet; and, on a dizzyingly narrow ledge overhanging the Reichenbach Falls, Holmes and Moriarty locked in hand-to-hand combat. Another column of images bordered the right-hand side, consisting this time of photographic portraits of the Conan Doyle specialists who had signed up for the Festival presumably well before I myself was asked. In fact, I was so belated an invitee that my own name went unlisted, and I couldn't help wondering whether, as is often the case with events planned long in advance, some more illustrious guest than I had dropped out at the last minute.

Of my five fellow speakers there were three with whom I was, to varying degrees, on nodding terms.

I knew Hugh Spaulding, a jocose, heavy-drinking, chain-smoking Dubliner, a former sportswriter on the *Irish Times*, who was the first to have been astonished by the small fortune he had made, and no sooner made had gambled away on 'the nags', out of a cycle of thick-ear thrillers each of which was set in a different professional sporting milieu. These thrillers all had titles so formulaic as to verge on provocation: e.g. *An Offside Murder*, *Death in the Scrum*, *Killer Mid-On*, *Bullseye!* and *To Live and Die on the Centre Court*, a novel in which the No 1 Seed is poisoned, in full view of thousands of spectators, during the fourth-set tie-break of a Wimbledon final. Tennis being the sole sport of interest to me, this latter book was the only one of his I had ever read. It was, though, enough for us to converse upon when I met him, a crumpled codger, now a self-confessedly impecunious has-been, with a can of lager in one hand and a minute battery-operated fan in the other, a fan whose open plastic rotor buzzed less than an inch away from his very veiny nose, at a mutual friend's birthday party one exceptionally warm August evening in a fairy-lit garden in Putney.

Hugh, I suppose, wasn't 'my kind of person'. But, as in sex, so also in the most superficial friendships, one finds oneself on occasion inexplicably drawn to somebody who isn't at all one's type. In any event, I rather liked him, and his book, and looked forward to catching up with him again.

A former acquaintance, too, was Pierre Sanary, who was down to speak on 'The Posthumous Holmes', which I interpreted to refer to the countless post-Doyle manifestations of the Great Detective in fiction, theatre and film, my own collection of stories perhaps included. Sanary was Swiss, widely travelled but with a home, if I'm not mistaken, in Geneva. He spoke an English so impeccably unstilted that to the English themselves it sounded haughty and condescending, as if every perfectly calibrated cadence were a rebuke to their risibly imperfect French. Stupendously erudite, an editor, publisher, anthologist, literary historian and I know not what else, he had written a series of monographs on such *petits-maîtres* of primitive pulp fiction as Jean Ray, Ernest Bramah, Sax Rohmer and Edgar Rice Burroughs, as well as a two-volume, thousand-page history of the whodunit, *Poë et Cie: Histoire du roman d'énigme de Poë au postmoderne*,* which covered all the usual suspects or, rather, all the usual detectives: Dupin, Lecoq, Holmes, Father Brown, Hercule Poirot, Harry Dickson, Nick Carter, Gideon Fell, etc. He was also the author of a single whodunit of his own, one I wish I had written.

Titled simply and superbly *Fin* – the English translation, *The End*, although both literal and unavoidable, forfeits half the original's clipped concision – it revolves around a group of American whodunit writers. One of them, we soon discover, is a serial killer, and all of them are in frantically competitive pursuit of the 'legendary' twist ending that was

---

* Published in Britain, considerably abridged, as *Poe & Co: A History of the Mystery Novel from Poe to Po-Mo* (Carcanet, 2003).

supposedly mentioned in passing by Poe in one of his letters to Hawthorne but never used by him because he never could think of a plot to which it would constitute the logical conclusion. Needless to say, at the end of *Fin* itself, at the very moment the serial killer discovers the nature of the twist, so equally, to his own rage, is revealed the utter futility of his quest, since the brilliantly original method by which he himself has contrived to dispose of his rivals is shown to be exactly that which was posited by Poe.

In, I would say, his early fifties, the totally bald Sanary resembled, with his poached-egg eyes and pale thin legalistic lips, a transvestite whose wig has just been snatched off. I had met him through my close friendship with the Chilean, Paris-based film director Raoul Ruiz, who had long and in vain nurtured the project of a cinematic adaptation of *Fin*. We had both been invited to supper at Raoul's flat near the Père-Lachaise cemetery and, even if Sanary displayed scant interest in anything I contributed to the table-talk and none at all in what I had achieved in my professional life, he himself proved to be so amazingly incapable of making a dull remark I could almost forgive his boorish manners. He had an inexhaustible pool of anecdotes and allegations involving instances of witting or unwitting aesthetic plagiarisms which he would serve up to us with a series of meaningful leers. He informed us, for example, that the out-of-control-carousel climax of Hitchcock's *Strangers on a Train*, absent from Patricia Highsmith's source novel, had been appropriated,

34

soi-disant 'Hitchcockian' touches and all, from Edmund Crispin's donnish Oxford-set whodunit *The Moving Toyshop*, published in 1945 and therefore predating the film by six years. Also that the plot of Cocteau's pretty much forgotten boulevard play *Les Monstres sacrés* (1940) was too similar to that of the still remembered and indeed cherished Joseph L. Mankiewicz film *All About Eve* (1950) for it to have been a coincidence. Also, most intriguingly, that in the first movement, with a reprise in the third, of a Sonata for Violin and Piano composed in the twenties by the Russian-born pianist and conductor Issay Dobrowen there can be heard a tune indistinguishable from 'As Time Goes By', which was reputedly conceived a decade later by one Herman Hupfeld and of course immortalised in the film *Casablanca*.

As for another of the Festival's invited speakers, Meredith van Demarest, I cannot honestly say that it was with much enthusiasm that I anticipated meeting her again. A hellish Hellenist from an obscure Californian college, she had sat next to me at a lunch in Antibes to which I had been invited by friends of friends many years ago, all the other guests being left-wing American academics spending their sabbaticals in sexy France rather than in dreary England, even though it was the latter country's language and literature most of them were being paid to teach.

She and I had got on well enough to begin with, in a discussion about some new French films which had just been released after the long hot hiatus of summer. Yet, even then, I couldn't quite suppress the conviction that the almost over-played attention she paid to my opinions derived not from any intrinsic interest they held for her but from her own avid consumption, to which she had slightly shamefacedly admitted, of gossipy literary biographies. My belief was that what she extrapolated from these was above all the fact that the secret of their subjects' success as conversationalists had resided less in what they themselves had had to say, however witty, than in the flattering intensity with which they had attended to the discourses, however trite, of their gratified interlocutors. Thus, whenever it was my turn to speak, she would peer into my eyes as though nothing in the world mattered more to her at that instant than my recommendation of Resnais or Rohmer (Eric not Sax).

Since this was 2001, however, and mid-September to boot, the conversation had inevitably turned to the Twin Towers attack, which had taken place just five days before. Speaking about the atrocity and its global implications – and I acknowledge I was a touch, shall we say, premature – I had bemoaned the fact that the military reprisals we all knew would follow were at the mercy of a buffoon of a politician the like of whom not even the United States, never a nation famous for voting its intellectuals into power, had known.

For a moment the table was silent. Then Meredith suddenly screeched at me:

'You little shit!'

'*What* did you say?' I managed to stammer out.

'Who fucking gave you the right to insult our President?'

Our President? George Bush? Would I be caught dead calling Tony Blair 'our Prime Minister'? And this from a self-styled radical left-winger.

'But all I said was –'

'Oh, can it!' she spat at me. 'I don't have to listen to such Eurotrash garbage!' Pulling a hundred-franc note from her purse, she tossed it onto the chequered tablecloth – 'That'll cover what I had!' – stood up and stalked alone out of the restaurant.

If everyone present was as startled as I was by her behaviour, one of her compatriots did coldly chide me for having been flippant, which was simply not true, about an event of such magnitude, and actually went so far as to pro-pose the eccentric theory that, the instant those planes ploughed into the Twin Towers, George Bush, ex-drunk, ex-deserter, ex-all-round-loser, had been alchemically transmut-ed into the Platonic essence of Presidential resolve. Whatever, the meal never recovered from Meredith's *coup de théâtre*. Just fifteen minutes later, we all quietly and sheepishly trooped out of the restaurant without dessert or coffee.

Several years, of course, had elapsed since the Towers crumbled to dust, and one had to suppose that, like so many liberal Americans who had put their critical faculties on hold, Meredith had since had time and cause to qualify her once unreflecting support for the cross-eyed cretin in the White House. But what mystified me was why she had not only been invited to but had herself agreed to attend what promised to be a frivolous Conan Doyle bash. Then, glancing at her minuscule bibliography, I learned from it that she had recently published a 'much-acclaimed' book-length essay titled *From Shylock to Sherlock* and subtitled 'Judaism, Patriarchy and the Forensic Imagination'. Ah.

The fourth speaker listed was G. Autry, a name calculated to stimulate critical inquisitiveness, like 'B. Traven'. Nobody knew what the G. stood for, if anything. He had hardly ever been photographed (on the Festival's flyer his photo had been replaced by a generic black silhouette against a plain white background), in recent years he had certainly never posed for a camera, and all he let be known about himself was that he was *not* related to Gene Autry, a once well-known singing cowboy whose horse would regularly rear up on its hind legs like that of a Spanish monarch in an equestrian portrait by Velasquez while he himself spun a lazy lasso above his head as though blowing a smoke ring. I had naturally never met him – who had? – but I had tried to read one of his novels, a sadistic thriller in the James Ellroy mode set in the racist Arkansas of the fifties. I laid it down again unfinished when the praeternatural vividness of its violence started to haunt my dreams.

Oddly enough, Autry's work had always had a pulpy reputation until Sanary, of all people, published an eccentric defence of it with the amusing title *G. est un Autry.** It was that essay which had prompted me to give his fiction a go. But I had, I repeat, so hated the novel in question that I only half-read it and, again, I couldn't imagine why such a grouchy recluse would make one of his extremely rare public appearances at an insignificant Sherlock Holmes Festival in the Swiss Alps.

Fifth and last – or, rather, first – was Umberto Eco, no less. But when I noted the parenthesis *(unconfirmed)* after his name, I just knew he wouldn't turn up. And I was about to fold up the attachment and pay for my coffee when I remarked, so discreetly boxed-off from the body of the text as to suggest that the festival's organisers were consciously playing hard-to-get with the reader, the two words, in the smallest of block capitals, MYSTERY GUEST. Underneath them I read as follows: 'The Meiringen Sherlock Holmes Festival is proud to announce the presence of a Mystery Guest, one whose identity, like those of so many murderers in mystery novels, will be revealed to you all in the library, that of our famous Kunsthalle. Do not attempt to guess in advance who he or she will be. You will certainly be proved wrong!'

This sounded to me as though it might be fun, but the potential for disappointment was of course also great.

---

* A mischievous parody of the near-homonymous '*Je est un autre*' ('I is an other'), Rimbaud's seminal poetic manifesto of the schizophrenic bifurcation of personality.

Chapter Three

In the early morning grisaille of September 10, just as I was irritably about to ring up the local minicab firm to remind it of my existence, I was collected outside my flat and driven off to the hell-on-earth that is Heathrow.

There I queued for nearly half an hour among a crowd of vacationers at a British Airways Economy check-in counter, only to learn to my fury, for my e-ticket was irresponsibly mum on the matter and I had assumed that the Festival, like most of its kind, would cut corners where its less than A-list guests were concerned, that I had after all been booked into Business Class. Two long hours later, I was finally aboard the plane, waiting for it to taxi out to the runway. Beside me, occupying a single seat, cutely belted in by a single seatbelt, were a pair of cherubic little boys (their parents sat across the aisle), just out of babyhood, identical twins identically dressed, chattering their heads off in American accents – Mid-West was my guess – as though compensating for all those months when neither of them could talk. It was distracting, and continued to be distracting during the flight itself – as always on plane journeys, I'd brought with me a computerised chess set and was forced, in order to give myself a decent chance in spite of the racket, to lower the machine's own level of skill a notch or two, with the result that its game instantly went off – but I really didn't mind. The chatter of my two little neighbours was so adorable that, had I not feared arousing parental suspicion, I would have joined in.

At Zurich a jewel-bright sky dazzled the airport's multiple glass façades. I was met by the Festival's director, Thomas Düttmann, in his late twenties, hence quite a bit younger than I had expected, preppily bow-tied and tousle-haired, with (like a lot of total strangers, I tend to find) one physical idiosyncrasy that took some getting used to: in his case, a nervous tic in the left eye whose beat accelerated in tandem with what I would later discover were intermittent fits and fevers of excitability. He shook my hand and relieved me of my suddenly inadequate-looking sole piece of luggage, a battered metal valise. At his side stood Hugh Spaulding, who had arrived twenty minutes earlier from Gatwick and struck me as even veinier and more crumpled than I remembered him. He sported (the appropriate verb) a bookmaker's checked, three-piece, almost parodically Irish tweed suit and a tie patterned with miniature huntsmen hallooing every which way, more than half of them upside-down. Over his right shoulder was slung a drab fawn mac, and a pair of bulging overnight bags sat at his feet. He remembered me too, greeting me with a beery 'Hello, Gil, long time no see.' He was smoking, and I accepted a cigarette from him, my first in the four hours of the trip. Then we climbed into a waiting Mercedes, Hugh and I together in the roomy back, Düttmann in the front seat next to the driver, and set out on what was to be the spectacularly scenic route to Meiringen.

Along the way Düttmann told Hugh and me that, like all the Festival's guests, we were to be put up at the Sherlock Holmes Hilton.

'It is not, I think, the best hotel in town,' he said to us over his shoulder. 'Oh, very nice, but three stars only. Its name, you know, was what you British call the "clincher". How could we resist the name?'

He explained, superfluously for Hugh but not for me, since I hadn't been listed in the Festival's emailed flyer as one of its speaking guests, that I would be 'on' that very evening, Hugh the next day after lunch. So far, he said, his eye blinking softly, it had all been a great success. And since we had quite a lot of free time before the evening's events, possibly we would like, once we had checked in and freshened up, to visit Meiringen's famous Museum.

'It is a must. Near the hotel and displaying choice exhibits which will please you both, I am sure.'

Staring moodily out of the window at an unending succession of mountainside chalets – I reckoned he already had a craving for another cigarette – Hugh offered a grunted affirmative, while I, a tactful old pro who knew what was expected of me, said that that sounded a very nice idea.

'But, Herr Düttman –'

'Please call me Thomas.'

'Thomas. I wondered when we'd be able to see the Reichenbach Falls.'

'Tomorrow afternoon, sir. We shall go together after Mr Spaulding's talk. A grand excursion has been arranged and the Mayor of our town has consented to make a speech.'

'Just one thing more. I noticed you referred to this evening's "events" – events in the plural. Does that mean another writer is also due to give a talk tonight?'

He shook his head. Immediately following my reading there would be a special screening of *Sherlock Holmes and the Spider Woman*, a film with 'the immense British actor Basil Rathbone', which neither of us was obliged to attend. 'Indeed,' he added, 'I am afraid you will be obliged *not* to attend for, while it is being shown, we plan a dinner for all our guests in a fine restaurant, followed by some nightclub dancing.'

I replied that I had seen the film, and it was evident that Hugh, who had ceased to contribute much to the conversation, cared only for a fag.

'Has the Mystery Guest arrived?' I asked.

'Not yet. We have not been informed exactly when he [so it was a he] is due. But we have organised a formal reception in his honour tomorrow morning at eleven o'clock in the Kunsthalle. Our Mayor will again be in attendance.'

'And Umberto Eco?'

The tic again.

'Unfortunately, he could not be among us. An illness in the family, I believe.'

'H'm,' I muttered to myself as our car squeezed through the mountains. 'He's not at all superstitious, I see.'

'What's that you say, Mr Adair?'

'Oh, nothing,' I replied.

The Sherlock Holmes Hilton turned out to be far more *gemütlich* than Düttmann's bet-hedging phraseology had intimated. Although not inspiring when we first glimpsed it on the drive which led up to its forecourt – an anonymous-looking, not especially lofty skyscraper that I guessed had once been an apartment complex – it had an airy, high-ceilinged lobby that, in Britain, would certainly have earned it a fourth star. And, as comic relief, the reception desk was manned by a prissy middle-aged queen who at once trained his Gaydar eye on me when opening my passport at my name and birthdate in order to copy them into the register.

Also to my pleasant surprise, my room was actually a suite, its furniture pale and beigey, smelling immaculately of lavender soap and flowers. From its tiny balcony was visible, in one direction, the town of Meiringen itself and the mountains beyond; in the other, just about, the Reichenbach Falls. It had, moreover, that absolute essential, a deep full-length bathtub, in which I hurriedly showered before rejoining Düttmann and Spaulding downstairs for our visit to the Museum.

The only drawback as I could see at short notice, but it was one I had anticipated, was the bed. It was of the Continental bolster-and-duvet type, and I also anticipated an ordeal of tossing and turning even before I managed to fall asleep, as my blind limbs tried to find just that posture that would allow them to make sense of their surroundings during the night. Incidentally, on each of its two rock-hard bolsters – it was a double bed – a gift-wrapped sweet had been laid. When I unwrapped one of them, I found a small meringue inside it. I at once thought 'meringue' and 'Meiringen' and how coincidentally close to anagrams of one another they were. It was no coincidence. According to the tourist booklet I leafed through before I finally quit the room, meringues had been invented in Meiringen. I live and learn.

The Sherlock Holmes Museum, too, was less dowdy, less provincial, than in my perhaps cynical and mean-spirited fashion I had expected. It was housed in the crypt of a deconsecrated English church right in the centre of the town, a town whose very Swiss stereotypicality I found conducive to reverie (even if the early-autumn absence of snow on its rooftops lent the whole compact little community the inconsolable air of a flock of freshly shorn sheep). There was, moreover, in the church's grassed-over grounds, a full-size bronze sculpture of Holmes reclining on a bronze park bench puffing bronze smoke from his bronze meerschaum; and affixed to the wall behind him was an oblong London-style street plaque which read: Conan Doyle Place, Borough of Meiringen.

Oddly, the Museum itself had been left unattended, its rackety little box-office empty. Anybody could walk in, so we did. And it was indeed worth a visit, even if it wasn't a patch on its double, the official London exhibit at 221b Baker Street.

The main attraction was a mocked-up replica of the cluttered living-room of Holmes and Watson's digs. Nothing had been forgotten: stuffy late nineteenth-century furnishings; conventional Victorian portraiture; a wall-full of framed snapshots of mostly ghostly oval photos of mostly ghostly oval faces; a sturdy *étagère* made of Japanese birch-wood; the mahogany desk at which one visualised Watson writing up his case histories; a bust, incongruously, of Conan Doyle himself; Holmes's violin, music-stand, pipes and pipe-rack (although not a hint of the picturesque para-phernalia of his cocaine addiction); a cartoonishly oversized magnifying-glass; a deerstalker cap (does Conan Doyle ever mention Sherlock wearing one? Must check up on that); a blood-tipped arrow (why?) on a half-moon table which had been shoved up against one of the walls; a luridly jacketed copy of *His Last Bow* lying as carelessly on the same table-top as if abandoned unread next to a faded edition of the *Daily Telegraph* dating from the teens of the twentieth century; a cryptogram we had neither the time nor inclination to set our minds to; and an evocative miscellany of small and stylish personal effects.

Thirsting for a coffee, we gave the museum shop a miss.* Instead we repaired, as Holmes would have put it, to a nearby café, where I at once recognised Sanary already scrutinising our approach from one of its white terrace tables. In front of him was an exotic pink cocktail, which he was stirring with a swizzle stick, and a rolled-up copy of the *Neue Zürcher Zeitung*.

'I fancy I know where you've been,' he said to Düttmann before the latter had time to make the introductions. 'The Museum, *n'est-ce pas?*'

He boorishly pretended to take a moment or two to recall who I was, gave Hugh an expansive handshake, congratulated him on his novels, which I found hard to believe he had ever read, and gestured for us to join him.

I asked him what he was drinking.

---

* Slightly to my regret, for I never tire of watching how bored tourists, most of whom have lost or else never mastered the art of meaningfully engaging with an exhibition of cultural artefacts in a museum setting, suddenly come alive again in the adjacent souvenir shop, purchasing the tawdriest trinkets and postcards with a gleeful gusto which contrasts conspicuously with the listless respect they have just shown inside the galleries themselves. Shopping is the only real, fully functioning culture left to us.

'It's called a Pink Negro. Vermouth, curaçao, pomegranate juice and a dash of Angastura bitters. Sounds horrible, I know, but the name enchanted me.'

Then, being a man possessed of no small talk whatsoever, he plunged directly into just the kind of learned literary chat I wasn't ready for, interesting as I knew it would almost certainly be.

To give you a sampling: our conversation having turned to Graham Greene, a writer for whom he, Sanary, had no time or patience ('Only the British could ever have regarded him as Nobelisable'), Hugh, who seemed to have decided up to that point that he was out of his depth, suddenly spoke up.

'No, no, old boy, you're wrong there. I don't like to be caught pulling rank, etc, etc, but if it's true only the British thought he should have won the Nobel Prize, it's because only the British are capable of appreciating his genius. You say he didn't have a personal style, etc, but what you don't get is that he had the kind of style that doesn't call attention to itself.'

'Pah!' snorted Sanary. 'It doesn't exist, this "style" that doesn't call attention to itself. It's just a threadbare old alibi you Brits employ to justify the insipidity and impersonality of your writers. I imagine that, for you, Somerset Maugham had a "style that doesn't call attention to itself". Am I right? Or J. B. Priestley, for Peter's sake.'*

Hugh mulled this over for a few seconds.

---

* Sanary's English was very good but thankfully not quite perfect.

'At least you won't deny Greene had a super gift for dialogue. Ever see *The Third Man*?'

'Yes, I did.'

'Good film, wouldn't you say?'

'Yes,' Sanary cautiously replied, 'it's a good film. Not the masterpiece the British seem to think it is, but, I agree, very entertaining.'

'Well, you remember, etc, etc, it had this big speech about Switzerland? On the Ferris Wheel?'

I was about to interrupt, to point out to Hugh, in spite of being on his side of the fence, that if film scholars were to be credited the speech he was visibly about to recite was now known not to have been Greene's contribution at all, when I was pipped at the post by Sanary himself.

'"In Switzerland they had brotherly love, five hundred years of democracy and peace, and what did that produce? The cuckoo clock." Am I right?'

'Yeah, that's it.'

'Actually, my dear Spaulding, that speech was written by Orson Welles, not Greene. Not to mention that it was already a plagiarism from James McNeill Whistler's *The Gentle Art of Making Enemies*. And I have to tell you, witty as it is, it does suggest that neither Whistler nor Welles knew very much about my country.'

We were all puzzled by this assertion, Düttmann included.

'Everybody thinks cuckoo clocks are Swiss,' Sanary went on. 'They're not. Oh, we Swiss are happy enough to fob them off on ignorant and credulous tourists. But in reality they come from the Tyrol. The Austrian Alps? So you see, my friends, it wasn't Switzerland with its five hundred years of democracy which produced the cuckoo clock. It was Austria, the land of Adolf Hitler.'

'What does that prove?' I asked.

'Nothing,' he replied with a shrug. 'Just as the speech in the film proved nothing.'

That was Sanary all over, an infuriating if always beguiling know-all. Except that he also had the unhelpful habit of not knowing when to stop.

'At least,' he said, barely drawing breath, 'at least Welles had the decency to make mention of democracy and brotherly love. Now Hitchcock – he was much worse.'

I looked at him quizzically.

'Come come, Gilbert, I refuse to believe you haven't read Truffaut's book of interviews with Hitchcock.'

'Yes, of course I have.'

'Indeed, you must have done. You parodied it, did you not, in your novel *A Mysterious Affair of Style*. Well, don't you remember what Hitch said about *Secret Agent*, his adaptation of Maugham's Ashenden stories?'

Already tiring of his oneupmanship, I shook my head.

'I quote [but how did he quote? Did he have a photographic memory?]: "One of the interesting aspects of the picture is that the action takes place in Switzerland. I said to myself, 'What do they have in Switzerland?' They have milk

50

chocolate, they have the Alps, they have village dances, and they have lakes. All of these natural ingredients were woven into the picture."

'*Mais quel con!* Natural ingredients? Milk chocolate? Village dances? *Village dances??* And Truffaut, *cet autre con*, instead of suggesting, oh ever so politely, ever so deferentially, that one might have the right to expect a filmmaker of Hitchcock's stature either to invert or, better still, avoid outright such whiskery old clichés, can only reply, *imbécile* that he is, "That's why the spies have their headquarters in a chocolate factory!" And this is what the French affect to think of as advanced theory? What a couple of blockheads! No? No? True? Faux?'

Then, before I knew how it happened, his monologue had turned again – for Sanary there existed no such thing as a *non sequitur* – to a trio of musical themes, from Puccini's *Gianni Schicchi*, d'Indy's *Symphonie sur un Chant Montagnard Français* and Casella's *Triple Concerto for Violin, Cello and Piano*, all three of which he hummed for us there and then to demonstrate how the composer Bernard Herrmann had purloined them for a few of his best-known scores for Hitchcock's films. To listen to him, the history of art, of all the arts, was nothing but an unending charge-sheet of theft and countertheft.*

---

* For a comprehensive inventory of these Herrmannian borrowings, see Sanary's article 'The Love Song of J. Alfred Hitchcock', *Sight and Sound*, volume 18, issue 4, April 2008.

He mentioned too, now almost as an afterthought, that not the least of the many logical absurdities in *North by Northwest*, one of the three films, incidentally, whose soundtrack scores he had exposed as second-hand, were the green and improbably symmetrical woods that Cary Grant and Eva Marie Saint traverse on their way to the monumental kitsch of Mount Rushmore.

'I took it upon myself to investigate,' he declared. 'There are no such woods,' adding cavalierly, 'not, of course, that that matters a jot.'

Düttman, meanwhile, was delighted not just that his eminent guests had taken no time at all to live up to their reputations for argumentative opinionation but also, somewhat contradictorily, that they were all getting on so well together.

As the conversation drew to an end, and Düttmann settled the bill, I was suddenly distracted by an irridescent soap bubble that wafted by my left ear and threatened to pop on the tip of my nose. Then another, and another, then a big fat one, then lots of delicately dainty little ones bumping and bursting against each other: it went on for so long I almost began to wonder if it could be some new, charming and as yet unrecorded species of weather. Turning my head to track it to its source, I noticed at another of the café's terrace tables, but as far away from us as it was possible to be, the cherubic twins from the flight. Each of them, ignoring the glass of orangeade which stood on the table before him, was blowing a rash of pixilated burps and borborygmi out through a minute eye-glass on a stick. As on the plane, their parents sat apart, intently discussing some matter of import. They too left their coffees untouched and, from time to time, one of them would good-humouredly swat a bubble. Were they in Meiringen, I wondered, for the Sherlock Holmes Festival? It didn't appear likely. But what other reason could there be?

Back in my room, I relaxed for an hour in the tub, before pulling the plug to let the slowly receding bathwater perform a soapy striptease over my recumbent nakedness. Then, feeling much refreshed, I strolled down to the Künsthalle, which was only a ten-minute walk from the hotel, and in its bar met up with Düttmann, Hugh, looking sprucer but with something on his mind, Sanary, who had changed into another, almost identical black blazer, the taciturn G. Autry, who, wearing jeans, a hyper-virile denim jacket and a shapeless Stetson hat in spite of being unrelated to singing cowboy Gene, addressed the one word 'Hi' to me, a few hovering members of the Festival's youthful 'creative team' who, I couldn't help noticing, outnumbered us guests three to one, and Meredith van Demarest.

I take no pleasure in coming clean – as I failed to do, deliberately, I suppose, when I first mentioned her name in this memoir – but, physically, Meredith was a stunner. Like all of us, she wasn't as young as she used to be – in her mid-forties, most likely – and there was a slightly brassy quality to her slick long blond hair and a glazed Valley vacuousness to her face, which was also blond if you know what I mean. But there could be no denying the fact that that face was almost boringly perfect in form and feature, with its pale tan complexion, sharply highlighted cheekbones and two unexpectedly pitch-black eyebrows. (Was her hair dyed or was it her eyebrows?) Or that her figure caused the long since obsolete, now politically incorrect, expression 'vital statistics' to swim up to the surface of one's memory. She was also tall, far taller than me and, as I watched her swan through the bar of the Kunsthalle towards us, I thought of a blowsily voluptuous B-movie actress whose initials she shared, Mamie van Doren, with the crucial difference that Meredith was an academic, not a film star, a fact which somehow rendered her all the more eyeball-distendingly sexy. As for her behavioural charm, it was, I repeat, of the drawly, eyelash-batting type which is always called 'disarming' but which instantly puts me on my guard.

'Gilbert . . .' she said softly. 'After all these years . . .'

'Meredith.'

'So how are you?'

'Oh, you know. How is anybody these days?'

'Mmmm.'

She turned to Düttmann, who took her dry martini off a waiter's tray and passed it over to her.

'Thank you so much. You probably didn't know this, Tommy, but Gilbert and I are old acquaintances.' (Her 'probably' she pronounced as a drawn-out 'praaahhhly'.)

'Really? You and – no, I confess I did not know that.'

'We first met several years ago. Antibes. The French Riviera. How long ago would it have been, Gilbert?'

I had been straining to read what was written on a curiously shaped brooch – of a snake swallowing its own rear end – pinned onto one of the lapels of her grey slim-waisted cotton jacket, and it was only after I had at last made out the words (I think) 'For All The Women of America' that I replied to her question.

'Actually, Meredith, if you think about it, it's an easy enough calculation. You recall, it was just after September 11. A matter of days after, if I'm not mistaken. So: September 15, 2001, let's say, to September 10, 2011. A decade almost to the day.'

'And what a decade it was,' observed our host.

Meredith smiled. Perfect teeth, natch.

'You must understand, though, Tommy, that that first meeting of ours was not a success.'

'No?'

'No. We definitely didn't hit it off. I have no desire to re-open old wounds but, as Gilbert rightly remembers, it was just after 9/11 and we were all good, patriotic, united Americans then, and to hell with our ideological quarrels. And no wonder. We thought it was the end of the world, and we wanted a President who would tuck us into our beds with a promise that the bogey man wouldn't come and murder us in the night. It sounds kind of puerile now, even babyish, but it was real scary back then and I'm afraid Gilbert just didn't get it. I can't blame him any more – nobody who wasn't American could have got it – and it was a long time ago and some of the things he said then, things that seemed obnoxious to me, have since come to make better sense – though if something's true now it doesn't necessarily mean it was always true, right? Anyway, even though it took us longer than all of you to see through that asshole President of ours, we finally did. My God, we finally did! As another President once said, you can fool some of the people all of the time, and all of the people some of the time, but you can't fool all of the people all of the time.'

I was half-expecting Sanary to inform us that the original of the Lincoln quote could actually be traced back to Chaucer, say, or *The Faerie Queen*; but, if he had such a notion, he was given no opportunity to share it. One of the 'creative team' discreetly raising a wrist, and a purple Swatch wristwatch, to Düttmann's eyes, the latter requested us all to please finish our drinks and proceed to the lecture hall, where we were awaited by an expectant full house.

Chapter Four

The house *was* full. While the others were shown to a half-dozen reserved end-of-row seats, one of which, Umberto Eco's I suppose, remained empty throughout, Jochen and I manoeuvred our tiptoeing way to the platform along a centre parting in which a half-dozen young people sat cross-legged on the wooden floor with bottles of mineral water on their laps. No applause as yet. Jochen spread his notes in front of him, tapped the microphone and, without, as they say, further ado, started to introduce me in German. Some laughter (I don't know why), a smattering of applause at the end. He turned to me with an encouraging smile. I removed my glasses – I look better with but read better without them – opened my much-fingered copy of *The Unpublished Case-Book of Sherlock Holmes*, took a last unfocused look round the hall, lowered my gaze and began:

'It has long been an axiom of mine,' said Sherlock Holmes, wearily glancing up from the formidable web of beakers and test-tubes which seethed and bubbled before his eyes, 'that it is when we indulge ourselves in some pursuit of pure relaxation, not when we are at our labours, tedious and repetitive though they may be, that we are most receptive to the gnawing torments of ennui.'

I turned my head in his direction. Having just re-entered the lodgings in Baker Street that we shared, from several hours passed at the bedside of a gravely ill patient of mine, I had at once buried myself in the day's newspapers, perusing them from cover to cover, and had in consequence paid little attention to either my companion or his activities. I contemplated him now. He had evidently chosen to perform one of his amateur experiments with acids and sulphates and, as was all too often true of his intense but also intensely volatile temperament, had come to tire of the pastime with the same sudden swiftness as he had undoubtedly embarked upon it. I myself could have asked at that moment for no more than to continue reading the news without interruption; but, being made belatedly aware that my day, although fatiguing in its exertions and still uncertain as to its outcome, had been filled with incident, I was bound to observe the soundness of his observation.

'Consider, for instance, my own case,' Holmes broodily went on, as he took down from the pipe-rack by the fireside what looked to be the oiliest and most ancient of his extensive collection of clay pipes and viciously tapped the dottle into the grate. 'Here have I been, today, with all the leisure in the world to do with as I pleased, to commence the monograph I have been planning to write on the significance of the typewriter key in modern detection or else' – and with his languidly tapering forefinger he indicated the instruments arrayed in front of him – 'undertake this amiable if futile little experiment. And yet, I swear, time has hung far heavier on my hands than on those of the potboy or crossing-sweeper who, since he awoke this morning, has assuredly done nothing but curse the drudgery of his quotidian round. No, my dear Watson,' he concluded, shaking his head, which was already enhaloed by a cloud of noisome tobacco fumes, 'it is some holiday excursion, or at the racecourse, or at the Opera when neither Madame Tetrazzini nor the divine Melba is singing – it is there, I say, that we learn to our cost what boredom truly means!'

Long experience had taught me to recognise the symptoms. Only a few days before, Holmes had brought to a satisfying conclusion a sordid affair of blackmail involving as its innocent party one of the noblest, most exalted names in England, and he was at present feelingly aware of his idleness.

'You have overtaxed yourself of late,' I said. 'Perhaps such enforced inaction is a blessing in disguise.'

'Bah!' he practically snarled at me. 'If there is one thing I abominate, it is a blessing in disguise. Surely blessings of any kind are sufficiently uncommon not to have to don a mask? Besides, it is not a blessing in disguise of which I stand most in need, but a criminal in disguise. Alas! The whole city of London appears to have reverted to "the straight and narrer", as our good Lestrade enjoys putting it. Where are they now, the Napoleons of crime? Languishing on Elba, I dare say.'

'If they are, then it is you yourself you must blame, Holmes,' I returned good-naturedly, 'for you have been their Iron Duke.' Laying down my copy of the *Gazette*, I rose from the settee and stepped over to the window to draw the curtains. It was an evening in early autumn, grey and overcast but not yet dark; save for an occasional scudding cloud-ball, the dimmed lustre of the heavens was even and neutral-tinted. At once attracting my eye, however, was a gentleman of somewhat cadaverous aspect who stood on the pavement opposite and who seemed quite overwhelmed by a heavy tweed overcoat which enveloped his thin frame like a bell-tent. In his left hand he held a small, unfolded piece of paper, and alternated between consulting it and peering up at the succession of house-numbers which confronted him. At last, having located the number he was searching for (as I surmised), he picked up the travelling-bag which had been sitting on the pavement beside him, crossed the street with a forthright stride and soon quit my view altogether.

'Well, I fancy your Calvary is at an end,' I remarked, 'for, unless I am much mistaken, the bell will ring this very minute to announce a new client.'

Holmes growled churlishly from the depths of his armchair. 'A client, is it? Most likely the distraught owner of a terrier gone missing from Kensington Gardens.'

'We shall soon find out,' I replied: 'here he is now.'

In effect, the front doorbell had already chimed, two sets of footsteps were to be heard on the stairs, and an instant later Mrs. Hudson was ushering into our room the very gentleman I had spied in the street below.

At a first glance, the man who stood before us was somewhere in his fifties. The almost military erectness of his bearing was impaired by a slight but perceptible stoop in his shoulders. From each side of his head, which was totally bald at the middle, protruded a shapeless tuft of white, fleecy hair resembling the stuffing from a mattress. And, divested as he now was of his generously sized overcoat, he could be seen to be most amazingly lean and bony, with facial features so near-skeletal that, taken along with his keen, lively eyes and unexpectedly warm skin colouring, I thought of a death's-head with a lighted candle posed inside it.

Since Holmes had not yet thrown off his fit of petulance, and appeared disinclined to do the honours, it was I who went forward, presented my companion and myself, and invited our visitor to take a chair.

'My dear sirs,' he murmured apologetically, 'you must forgive me for intruding on your intimacy unannounced, and at this late hour, but I . . . I truly am at my wits' end. If I had known where else I might turn, I assure you I would never have presumed to disturb you. Oh, but here I am so far forgetting myself that I have failed to offer you my card.'

'And yet, even as you are, you are not entirely a stranger to us,' said I. 'Am I not right, Holmes?'

'Why,' said our visitor, perplexed, 'what can you mean? To my recollection, we have not met before.'

'I mean only,' I answered, eager this once to exercise my own powers of deduction, 'that you are obviously left-handed and a former Army officer, that you have a brother of far stockier physique than yourself and that, having lived in Devon for a good many years, you are naturally unfamiliar with our metropolis.'

'But, bless my soul, sir, you astonish me!' he cried. 'I can hardly believe –'

'Oh,' I said lightly, 'it was really very elementary, you know. Your left-handedness you gave away when –'

'Dr. Watson,' he interrupted me in no little degree of agitation, 'if I say you astonish me, it is that I am in fact right-handed, I have never been a soldier, I was an only child, I have had to visit London four times this past fortnight and, far from living in Devon, I've not once set foot in the place!'

For a moment or two there was a disconcerting silence; then, to my relief, Holmes suavely intervened.

'My friend Watson here,' he said, 'whom it has amused to chronicle a few of my trifling successes, has, as you may observe, his own rather underhand method of enquiry. To wit, by postulating the exact contrary of what he senses to be true, he hopes to elicit all the requisite information at once.' He yawned. 'It sometimes works.'

'Most . . . most ingenious,' responded our visitor, although, to judge by his prolonged scrutiny of me, his doubts as to my competence, and possibly even my sanity, were by no means allayed.

'But to your problem,' Holmes went on. 'You are, I think, Dr. Eustace Gable, one of our most esteemed botanists. Oh, be assured,' he drawled, seeing his interlocutor about to speak, 'it is through no process of ratiocination that I have identified you. It happens that I recently attended an event at the Royal Botanical Society at which you read a most stimulating paper on the variety and luxuriance of South American fronds.'

'Fronds are my passion, Mr. Holmes!' Gable said fervently. 'And, in a way, it is that passion that has brought me here tonight.'

'Pray continue,' said Holmes, placing the tips of his fingers together and pensively propping his chin upon them.

'I should explain that I inhabit a large family estate called The Gables, by a curious coincidence, and situated halfway between Aylesbury and the village of Mentmore. The servants apart, the sole company I have in my rather lonely household are my sons James and Edward. They are not brothers, you understand, but half-brothers: my first wife died in childbirth, poor dear girl, and my second barely more than twelvemonth ago. Yet James and Edward have been as loving to one another as if they were indeed brothers, and their pranks have brightened many a winter evening for me.

'Now it's this way, Mr. Holmes. As I have said, I specialise, as a botanist, in those leaves characteristic of the palm or fern, and my enthusiasm has made of me a much-travelled man. There scarcely remains a corner of the globe to which I have not ventured in search of rare specimens, and I lately spent a fascinating two months in Sumatra in the Dutch East Indies. Well, exactly four weeks ago we docked at Southampton and the specimens I had had crated in Padang were forwarded to Aylesbury by the railway and then brought to the house by my man Jerrold in the dog-cart.

'It was on that morning that was set in motion the inexplicable train of events which prompted me to seek outside assistance. We were in the kitchen – my two boys and I, along with one or two members of the staff – watching Jerrold screw open the crates with a crowbar. And it was when we were starting to lay the fronds out on the fine tissue paper which I purchase and store for just that purpose that, with a frightful scream, Jerrold suddenly withdrew his bare arm from within one of the crates. Gathering about him, we were all aghast to find him bleeding copiously from a profound and horribly corrugated gash in his wrist. Although he has always been of a robust constitution, I own I was quite afraid for him: he had in a trice turned white, there was terror in his eyes and my foremost anxiety was that he was about to faint. However, the thing appeared so abruptly I had no more time to think about him.'

'The thing?' echoed Holmes, rousing himself at last from the apathy into which he had sunk and fixing Gable with a penetrating eye. 'What nature of thing?'

'The rat!' cried Gable.

'I beg your pardon?' said Holmes, now bolt upright.

'A rat, a giant rat!' Gable went on breathlessly. 'Oh, when I call it a giant, you must not infer from the term that there was anything supernatural about its size – I make this distinction now that you may better understand the import of what is to follow – but by the standard of our common-or-garden English rodents it certainly was disagreeably large. It darted from the crate, scurried across the kitchen floor and vanished out of the door leading to the main hallway.'

'But this rat,' I asked: 'where could it have sprung from?'

'Well, Dr. Watson,' Gable replied, 'when you collect and study fronds, you learn to expect the discovery of all kinds of living creatures, spiders, beetles and a few rather more outlandish insects, which have crept unnoticed inside the packing crates. But a rat, and of such a dimension! I can only suppose that the native bearers, who are lazy at the best of times, had been especially dilatory. The point, Mr. Holmes, is that this . . . this rat has poisoned my whole existence! Although I myself am persuaded that it must have made its way into the grounds, where it would soon have perished for want of its natural sources of nourishment, it has not ceased to cast an evil shadow over my house.'

'You interest me extremely,' said Holmes, refilling his pipe. 'Continue, do.'

'I know not if it is the animal itself or its legend that has since grown to monstrous proportions, but we have all, for a month now, heard queer nocturnal patterings under the floorboards as of some huge, restless beast on the prowl. Meat has been found, half-devoured and spat out in a corner of the pantry. And if these manifestations already had the servants quivering with dread, just above a week ago one of the scullery maids, on her way upstairs to bed, saw what she swears was an enormous rat, with bright yellow phosphorescent eyes and a head the size of a full-grown otter's, slithering across the first-floor landing! On that same night, too, as the first excitement was subsiding at last, there was a further alarum when Edward awoke to find the creature lurking in his bedroom.'

'And Jerrold?' Holmes asked. 'How has he fared?'

'Jerrold?' said Gable, seeming distracted by the question. 'Oh, he lay in a bad fever for several days but is now quite recovered. My worry is not with Jerrold. It is with servants who daily threaten to hand in their notice, with tradesmen who will no longer deliver their wares – the atmosphere in the household has become, as I say, poisonous, quite unbreathable. As a man of science, I refuse to lend credence to old wives' tales of phantom rodents with phosphorescent eyes, but I tell you something must be done or I shall go insane! Will you help me, Mr. Holmes?'

For a while Holmes reflectively rubbed his fingertips against his chin. He finally said, 'Well, Dr. Gable, it is a most interesting and *outré* story that you have told us. And though, notwithstanding my versatility, I have never before been hired as a rat-catcher, yes, I shall indeed take your case. What say you, Watson, are you game?'

Having done everything I could to make my patient as comfortable as was humanly possible for one in so touch-and-go a condition, I answered that I would be very pleased to join Holmes on this oddest of missions.

'Then how shall we proceed?' he asked his new client.

'I hardly dare impose upon you further,' said Gable hesitantly, 'but if it would not inconvenience you to accompany me to Aylesbury this very evening on the 8.15 from King's Cross, Jerrold will be waiting to take us on to The Gables.'

'Capital,' said Holmes. 'To Aylesbury it is.' And Mrs. Hudson was immediately instructed to prepare our bags.

The journey itself was uneventful. With Holmes immersed in a volume of Petrarch while Gable and I chatted about India, a land with whose mysteries we were both intimately familiar, we arrived at Aylesbury just after ten o'clock. And even if the station forecourt had not been deserted, I believe I should have recognised Jerrold from Dr Gable's description: he was indeed of robust build, his right arm still bandaged at the wrist and hanging more slackly than the other.

There was a dog-cart standing by and we at once set forth for The Gables.

Not three-quarters-of-an-hour had elapsed when, without any apparent prompting from Jerrold, the horse turned in at a pair of wrought-iron gates then imperturbably trotted up the driveway to the house. It was a starless night; but although most of The Gables' turreted façade was obscured in the enveloping gloom, I imagined I could make out a pinprick of light, as if from a waving lantern, directly in front of us. And so proved to be the case for, to our astonishment, before we had quite reached the main entrance, a wild-eyed young woman clad in a tartan dressing-gown, her hair all dishevelled, dashed forward into our path.

'Oh, Dr. Gable, Dr. Gable, thank God you've returned at last!' cried this apparition, swinging her lantern crazily from side to side.

'Why, Mary Jane,' rejoined Gable, nonplussed by her greeting. 'Calm yourself! What is the matter with you?'

''T'aint me, sir!' she screeched. ''Tis Master James, sir!'

'Master James?' said Gable, and he turned ashen-grey. 'What about Master James?'

'Oh, he's dead, sir! Killed, sir! Killed by the rat!'

Preceded by our guide, and by the lantern which swayed and pitched ungovernably in her trembling hand, we descended from the carriage and rushed inside the house. So hurried was our pace, and so dimly lighted the downstairs area, Holmes and I had next to no opportunity to note the style or disposition of its furnishings. For it was up two flights of a broad central staircase that Mary Jane led us, until we found ourselves in a dark top-floor corridor, at whose far end, assembled on the threshold of an open door-way, a tight little huddle of people were to be seen.

When we, in our turn, stood outside that open door, the spectacle we encountered was perhaps the most extraordinary that I have ever known, even in my long association with Sherlock Holmes.

The room itself was in the nature of an attic, stark and cell-like, higher than it was long, save where its ceiling sloped down to nearly the halfway mark of the wall furthest away from where we stood. It was very sparely equipped, its furniture consisting, for all in all, of a low, monkish cot, two cane chairs and a massive mahogany chest-of-drawers whose legs were curved and squat like those of a bull mastiff. Just above it, with perhaps a foot-and-a-half to separate them, was the room's only window, which was small, rect-angular and glassless, and crosscut by a pair of narrow iron bars.

But it was the awful sight of James Gable, a boy of some sixteen summers, which transfixed our gaze. He lay stretched out lengthwise on the cot in the exact pose, and with the same deathly pallor, of the dead Chatterton in Wallis's celebrated painting, except that his two hands tightly gripped his own neck and his naïve and youthful features had been warped out of shape by a grimace of ineffable and indescribable horror.

With a ghastly moan the boy's father made as if to fling himself on the cot, but Holmes, his lean frame suddenly exploiting that unexpected reserve of physical strength that has got the better of many a Limehouse bruiser, managed to hold him back.

'Courage, man, courage!' he cried. 'Something foul has taken place here, and it would be best if the lad were left undisturbed for now.' He turned to me. 'Watson, there is, I fear, little doubt as to the ultimate diagnosis, but examine him nevertheless. And do so, pray, without moving him. Watson? Are you unwell?'

'I am sorry, Holmes,' said I, and my voice quivered. 'It's . . . it's just that it is all so uncanny . . . like a stage-set. Forgive me.'

While Holmes continued to hold his client back by the shoulders, I quickly stepped over to the cot. Although no doubt remained that young James Gable was gone, I was obliged to prise his hands from off his neck to learn the precise cause of his death. And there I discovered a cut so deeply incised that it had utterly severed the jugular vein, a cut, as I observed to my consternation, corrugated in form –

just as Jerrold's was said to have been – and apparently effected by a row of huge razor-sharp teeth. Judging by the rictus on the youth's face, I supposed that he had expired both from that cut and from the abrupt heart failure which would have been its immediate consequence.

This startling information I conveyed to Holmes as succinctly as I could, and I saw his hollow cheeks flush with horror. He ran his eyes over the assembled servants – they were still standing in the doorway, shivering with fear yet continuing to stare at the macabre *tableau* inside the attic room – and finally let them settle upon a handsome, tow-haired, barefoot young man dressed in nothing but a long white nightshirt.

'You are Edward Gable, are you not?' he enquired of him.

'Yes, sir, I am,' the youth answered rather hoarsely, no doubt in awe of Holmes's masterful presence.

'How old are you, Edward?'

'Just passed eighteen, sir.'

'Now, my boy,' said Holmes, softening his tone, 'you realise, don't you, that your brother is dead?'

'I do, sir,' replied Edward, who, bar a faint trembling of his lower lip, allowed no expression of feeling to be visible on his face. 'It was… it was I who found him so.'

'Well, my name is Mr. Sherlock Holmes, and later I shall have to ask you and everybody else a number of important questions. But first, I think, your father should be comforted. Will you take him downstairs and pour him some brandy?'

'Yes, sir, I will.'

And, without a further word being spoken by either, he took his father by the arm and guided that now visibly broken man along the corridor and down the staircase.

Holmes meanwhile, facing the others, spoke to the oldest and most responsible-looking person there, a woman whose plump and kindly face was still streaked with the copious tears which she had already shed.

'You are . . .?'

'Mrs. Treadwell, sir. I am Dr. Gable's housekeeper, if you please,' replied this typical specimen of the housekeeping breed.

'I do not imagine, Mrs. Treadwell,' said Holmes, 'that anyone has had the mind to send for the police?'

'Why no, sir . . . that's to say . . . if you please, sir, it all happened so sudden . . .'

'Quite so. Then, Jerrold, may I suggest you take the dog-cart back to Aylesbury and alert the constabulary there.'

Tapping his cap respectfully with his bandaged hand, Jerrold left at once to carry out the request.

Holmes now closed the attic door. 'As for you young women,' he continued in his most authoritative manner, addressing Mary Jane and two other hysterically twittering maids, 'I propose that you go downstairs also, that you stay close together and await the arrival of the police from Aylesbury. Mrs. Treadwell, if you will remain behind, I would like to ask you a few questions.'

Once the maids had left, Holmes turned towards that good lady.

'Now, Mrs. Treadwell,' said he, 'it was Edward, I understand, who discovered his brother's body?'

'By rights, sir, it was him and me both.'

'How so? Please tell me everything that occurred and omit no detail, however insignificant it may strike you.'

'Well, sir, the facts are these. There's been a fearful state of affairs in this house ever since Dr. Gable's crates were shipped here and a horrid great rat –'

'Yes, I know all about that,' Holmes smoothly interrupted. 'I wish you to relate only what happened here this evening.'

'It's just that, because of the rat and the stories that were being spread of it, young Master James, who was such a lively boy, always full of humour, had of late sunk into a kind of terror. And this very evening, when we heard its scratchings louder than ever, he swore he wouldn't pass the night in his own bedroom – there being no lock on its door, you see – but would sleep in the attic, a room that no one ever entered or cleaned but could at least be locked from the inside. And that he did, sir, and turned the key behind him, at about half-past nine, I should say. Well, I was undressing in my own room when, no more than five or ten minutes after, I heard a scream coming from upstairs, a scream that changed me to stone, sir! I rushed out, just as you see me now, and I met Master Edward in the corridor, him only half-undressed himself. We came up here, and knocked on this door as loud as could be, but no answer was forthcoming. We cried, "Jamie! Jamie!" fit to wake the dead in Mentmore graveyard, but there wasn't a stirring from him.'

'And the door was locked from inside?'

'Oh yes, sir. We tried rattling it, but it wouldn't budge. At last Master Edward thought that it could be brought down by force – it was old and damp, sir, quite eaten up with rot – and it took just two heaves with his strong young shoulder to break it open. And there . . . Oh, Mr Holmes,' she said, now openly weeping, 'it was the most inhuman thing I ever saw . . .'

'Please bear up, Mrs. Treadwell. What happened next?'

The housekeeper endeavoured to gather her thoughts. 'Next . . .? Yes, Master Edward told me to go and wake Mary Jane that she might keep a lookout for Dr. Gable who, as we knew, was due back from London. I did wake the girl, and returned here within the quarter-hour to find him still standing watch at the door.'

'You did not examine James to make certain he was dead?'

'Master Edward did, and hoped to revive him too. But the boy was dead, sir, with not a breath of life left in him. And his face . . . If I live to be a hundred . . .'

'Yes, indeed, it is a terrible business. But you have been of the greatest assistance to me, Mrs. Treadwell, and I would ask you now to join the others downstairs.'

After she had taken her leave, Holmes smiled grimly. 'Well

now, Watson, let us, you and I, turn our attention to the scene of the crime. For I believe we'll have a clear run of an hour or more until the police arrive, and I am most anxious to explore the room before the hobnailed boots of the Aylesbury constabulary contrive to stamp out what evidence there yet may be.'

Inside the attic, Holmes undertook his investigation as coolly as if there had been nobody at all on the cot, let alone the mangled corpse of a once personable young lad whose expression of naked terror appeared to pursue me wherever I moved. The door, as Holmes ascertained, had indeed been forcibly burst open, and its key was still in the lock – on the inside. That key impressed me as being, so to speak, the key to the whole affair, for I could not conceive how either a human being or a rodent had entered and subsequently quit the room without in some fashion causing it to be disturbed. And it was then it occurred to me that, if the cot on which James was lying sat too low on the floor to conceal a man, there was certainly space enough for a rat still to be lurking . . .

At that moment Holmes, with a negligent disregard for his trouser knees, clambered atop the chest-of-drawers and peered out of the barred window.

'Interesting, by Jove,' said he, as, with remarkable agility even for him, he leapt back down on the floor.

'What is?' I asked, one eye warily on the cot.

'Running underneath the wall there appears to be a

stream, which doubtless serves as a drainage conduit for the house. Watson, have you something the matter with your eye?'

'Not at all,' I answered impatiently; then, mutely signalling my suspicion as to what might still be cowering under the bed, I said, 'There is, I suppose, absolutely nothing to this queer story of a rat?'

Holmes looked up at me interrogatively and managed the closest to a true smile that I had seen on his features since we had ventured into this tragic house.

'Your conjecture is,' he said, 'that the Sumatran rat is even now preparing to ambush us from beneath the bed?'

'No, no, of course not,' I muttered, none too convincingly, I fear. 'However, as I see it, no man could have left this room, but a small animal might have climbed on to the chest-of-drawers, crept out of the window and plunged into the stream below.'

'Precisely!' said Holmes in triumph. 'A *small* animal. Logic, man, logic! Oh, I grant you a giant rat might just have slain the boy – but then, it could no more have squeezed itself under the bed nor escaped by the window than I could. And no normal rodent capable of taking flight in the way you have just conjectured could ever have inflicted those teeth marks. No, Watson, instead of searching for major monstrosities, you should confine yourself, as I do, to minor oddities – such as this,' and he drew his forefinger along one of the floorboards and held up its tip for my inspection.

'Why,' I said upon examining it, 'I see nothing there.'
'That,' said Holmes, 'is the minor oddity.'

Nearly two hours elapsed before the police arrived from Aylesbury, in the person of an Inspector Cushing, who turned out to be a genial red-haired man in his middle forties with a tendency to stoutness, and who came accompanied by two uniformed constables. Just a few minutes after that, we were all discreetly conversing in the library, Holmes, Cushing and myself standing some way apart from the members of the household staff, most of whom were gathered about the pathetic figure of Dr. Gable. The poor man, he sat still and hunched in an armchair, his head lolling limply forward over his chest like that of an unstrung marionette.

This library was a dark, splendidly-proportioned room, three of whose walls were lined with tall bookcases and the fourth dominated by a superb Adam fireplace above which had been mounted the stuffed heads of a trio of magnificently antlered Highland stags. Sprawled in front of the blazing fire, a pair of cocker-spaniel dogs, so alike one to the other as to be surely twins, mournfully contemplated their master's distress.

Cushing, already conversant with Holmes's exploits, was more than amenable to the prospect of my friend assisting him in his inquiries. He had heard, too, of the story of the rat as, before he decided to seek help from farther afield, it was the Aylesbury police that Dr. Gable had originally approached with his strange narrative.

'Alas, Mr. Holmes,' said Cushing, 'I informed the Doctor that the matter which exercised him seemed hardly to fall under our domain. I even suggested that he send out for a rodent-killer such as are to be found in these farming areas. I realise now that I was too hasty in dismissing him and should have paid closer attention.'

'You cannot be faulted for having failed to anticipate such a fantastical crime as this,' answered Holmes, puffing on his briar. 'Besides which, I categorically assure you that, until this very night, you would not have found one solitary clue as to what was about to occur.'

'Why, Mr. Holmes,' said Cushing, staring at him open-mouthed, 'you are speaking as if you know exactly what lies at the heart of the mystery.'

'Scarcely that, Inspector. Naturally, I know who killed young James Gable, but I still have a very incomplete picture as to how the thing was done and no conception at all as to why.'

'Ah! And the rat?' asked Cushing, his tone now inflected with a touch of sarcasm. 'Would you be knowing where that might currently hide out?'

'The rat?' Holmes drawled. 'I haven't the faintest idea.'

I had been observing Holmes throughout this exchange and could not help noticing that, although he appeared to give all his attention to the Inspector, his gaze had almost imperceptibly begun to shift to some point above the other's head.

Suddenly, his face illumined from within, he slapped the palm of his hand against his brow.

'Blind, blind, blind!' he exclaimed. 'I have been here in this library for well-nigh two hours and I have observed nothing! And like every blind man I flattered myself that I was some kind of a seer. Well, *now* I know where the rat is!'

Once again he addressed himself to the police officer.

'Inspector Cushing, you were good enough to express a certain respect for my past successes in the forensic sciences, were you not?'

'That I was,' answered the other; 'and considerably more than "a certain respect", I'd like to add.'

'Then in the light of that respect will you now indulge me to the extent of lending me your carriage and one of your constables, and granting me no more than, shall we say, four hours to prove a point?'

'Well . . . yes, sir, I suppose I can do that if you believe it'll be of service to you,' said a puzzled Cushing.

'It will be of immeasurable service,' said Holmes. 'Mrs. Treadwell, if I may trouble you again,' he called over to the housekeeper.

She appeared at once before us.

'Please forgive me, Mrs. Treadwell, for trespassing further upon your time, but I should like to ask you two final questions.'

'Yes, sir?'

'First, do you know the name of Dr. Gable's solicitor?'

'That would be Mr. Hunter, sir, of Hunter and Dove in Aylesbury.'

'Excellent. Now – and I wish you to reflect very carefully before answering – when you returned upstairs to the attic bedroom after awakening Mary Jane, am I right in assuming that young James Gable had shed rather more blood than when you first saw him?'

The housekeeper did not wait to reflect. 'Why yes, sir!' she replied with a look of surprise on her corpulent features.'I didn't think of it again till this very minute, but there *was* more blood on the poor boy's nightshirt.'

'Then,' cried Holmes, 'the problem admits of only one solution and, if I may prevail upon you now, Cushing, for the man and the carriage that you have promised me, I feel certain I shall be able to disclose it to you before tomorrow morning is out.'

Holmes proved to be as good as his word. It was at sunrise that he set off from the house, to return exactly as the library clock was striking the tenth hour. Followed by the constable who had accompanied him on his enigmatic excursion – and who now carried a shapeless bundle wrapped up in a linen kerchief – Holmes invited Cushing and myself to join him in the billiard-room where we would be able to talk undisturbed.

On seeing how solemn his countenance was, in a chilling contrast to the barely suppressed excitement and even jubilation which I had read on his face as he departed, I ventured to remark that he had been disappointed in his mission.

'*Au contraire*, Watson,' he answered. 'It is only that I was so intoxicated by the thrill of the chase that I near forgot the implications of what I would uncover were I to be proved right.'

'And,' said the Inspector, his gruff voice betraying the profound curiosity he felt, '*were* you proved right?'

'I was, Cushing, I was, and when you have listened to what I have to say, I do not doubt that you will at once decide to arrest Edward Gable for the murder of his halfbrother James.'

The police officer was dumbfounded by this extraordinary statement, although not more so than I was myself.

'Unfortunately,' Holmes continued, 'it is the very truth. And my fear is that the poor father will take it badly, this blow following so soon upon the other.'

'Really, Holmes,' I expostulated, 'you owe us an explanation. For I believe I speak for Cushing here when I say that we are both utterly in the dark.'

'And yet, Watson, it was an astute observation of yours which first put me upon the scent.'

'Of mine?' I echoed incredulously, for I had the impression of having contributed next to nothing to his investigation.

'Yes, indeed. When faced with that ghoulish scene

upstairs, you likened it to a stage-set, as I remember. Well, that is precisely what it was, a stage-set, a *tableau vivant*, very possibly inspired by those for which our Baker Street neighbour Madame Tussaud is justly famous.'

'Not truly *vivant*, after all,' I demurred.

'Yet it was initially so,' retorted Holmes. 'But we ought to begin at the beginning. Never having been a devotee of Penny Dreadfuls, I at once eliminated the hypothesis of the rat. Rats, especially giant ones with phosphorescent eyes, tend to make footprints; and when I noted the complete absence of dust in a room that I was told was never occupied and never cleaned – the minor oddity, Watson, which I tried to call to your attention – I suspected that we must be dealing with murder, and a murder that was particularly cold-blooded in its execution.'

'Very well, but why Edward?' asked the Inspector.

'My suspicions of him were aroused almost at once. As you will recall, Watson, Mrs. Treadwell told us that, on hearing James's scream, Edward had rushed into the corridor partially undressed. Yet, when you and I arrived not more than half-an-hour later, we found him in nothing but his nightshirt. Now who, upon discovering his own sibling violently slain, would still go tranquilly about preparing for bed? No, Cushing, I fancy young Edward was obliged to remove his clothes in haste because they had become stained with his half-brother's blood, and you would do well to have one of your constables search his bedroom, as he certainly cannot have had the time to dispose of them.

'I had, then, a strong conviction as to the perpetrator of the crime: the riddle was understanding *how* it had been committed. But, in that, I let myself be guided by one of my principal articles of faith, which is – as my poor friend Watson is doubtless tired of hearing – that when you have excluded the impossible, that which remains, however improbable, must be the truth. And at once that truth revealed itself to me: *when Edward and the housekeeper burst into the attic, James Gable was alive*. It was only *after* Mrs. Treadwell departed, and the two brothers were left alone together, that he was murdered.

'Edward, I fear, had long been plotting how best he might rid himself of his half-brother. Despite being the elder son, he would not have inherited the family estate – as I learned this morning at Messrs. Hunter and Dove – because he is the offspring of the first Mrs. Gable, and the estate belonged, not to the doctor, but to his second wife, whose will specified that, in the event of her premature death, it should pass to James directly he attained his majority. You see, Watson, when Dr. Gable chanced to remark to us that his house was called The Gables "by a curious coincidence", he was telling us that its name had nothing to do with his own: he meant simply that, like many another so-called, it was gabled.

'Edward therefore waited for his opportunity, and it eventually presented itself in the guise of an implausibly large rodent that escaped from one of his father's packing crates and is perhaps even now, a bewildered and maligned innocent, roaming the Buckinghamshire countryside. The two brothers were fond of playing practical jokes together, as we were told by both Dr. Gable and Mrs. Treadwell, and I imagine that they were oftentimes heedlessly cruel, as young people's pranks will be. So, with the elder of the two taking upon himself the role of evil genius, they proceeded to foster the legend of a supernatural rat at large, with easily contrived scamperings under the floorboards and half-masticated chunks of meat in the pantry. As for the phantom creature which so terrified one of the maids, that, I specu-late, was one of Dr. Gable's cocker spaniels with its fore and hind legs roped together and its canine identity craftily concealed under some phosphorescent Hallowe'en mask.

'At any rate, the events of last night were to constitute the *pièce de résistance*, as it were, of the whole charade, in which James would be found "dead" in the attic, gored by the Sumatran rat, before leaping up with a triumphant grin on his face to be scolded and, I should say, almost at once forgiven for having frightened the household out of its col-lective wits. A callous hoax, no doubt, but not untypical of youthful high spirits.

'Alas for poor James, Edward had quite a different project in mind; and when, with the housekeeper's departure, he was all alone with his brother, he smothered the younger boy with the very pillow his head rested upon and tore deep and hard into the veins of his neck' – whereupon Holmes untied the bundle which the constable had brought in with him and which we saw to contain a large rock, a blood-stained pillow and the stuffed head of a wolf, its lower jaw snapped off so that just the vividly snarling upper teeth remained.

'Take care how you handle that,' Holmes warned the Inspector, 'for these fangs are far sharper now than when the beast still had his employment of them. In a sense, the whole case hinged upon the incisions made in James's neck, and it was only when, in the library, I found myself idly admiring the doctor's collection of mounted animal heads that it dawned on me how they might have been effected. In Aylesbury I did the round of its curiosity shops and learned in the third that Edward had recently purchased just such a head. Its teeth, as you may observe, he honed down until they had become as sharp and vicious as jack-knives. And it was of course with this pillow that he stifled his victim, having first stained it with the blood – most likely that of some rabbit or squirrel – which he had also smeared on James's neck to achieve the effect of a violent and sanguinary death. When the boy was murdered in earnest, he naturally shed more blood, as Mrs. Treadwell confirmed, real blood this time, his own.'

'And the rock?' I asked.

'It acted as ballast,' said Holmes. 'After committing the deed, Edward hastily wrapped his accessories up in a bundle and shoved them through the window into the stream below, whence the constable and I extracted them on our return from Aylesbury. They too would have been got rid of in due time.

'There you have the whole dreadful story,' he concluded. 'And now, Inspector, I fear it is my melancholy duty to advise my client as to the outcome of my investigation. Shall I leave you, then, to proceed with the arrest?'

That same evening, back in Baker Street, I was seated at my small writing-desk, busy composing a first draft of the case I had already decided to call 'The Giant Rat of Sumatra', while Holmes had gone to his violin, as was customary with him after some professional exertion, and had started to essay the opening bars of one of Paganini's more fiendishly intricate Caprices.

'I realise, Watson,' he suddenly said to me in a meditative tone of voice, 'how much you have enjoyed turning my case-book into a cycle of forensic romances, but I cannot help wondering whether, on this occasion, you might prefer to leave the crime private and unrecorded.'

'Whyever so?' said I, glancing up from my notes.

'Oh, it is simply that Eustace Gable is one of our most distinguished public men, and his life has been so blighted by this tragedy that I am afraid his constitution has been shattered beyond repair. It would surely be unworthy of us to advertise our success, but equally his ghastly plight, in the pages of a popular magazine.'

'Perhaps you are right, Holmes,' I answered after a

moment of reflection. 'And yet I am not resigned to giving it up altogether. What if I were to write it up now but stipulate that it remain unpublished for, let's say, a hundred years?'

Holmes plucked a frivolous little pizzicato on his bow-string.

'A hundred years? 2011?' He laughed. 'Oh, how you do exaggerate, Watson! I can assure you that in 2011 the name of Sherlock Holmes will have been consigned to the most complete and utter oblivion.'

In virtually everything – save, of course, those matters which pertain to my own professional skills – I readily acknowledge my friend's superior acumen. In this instance, however, I fancy he might be mistaken.

Chapter Five

The applause was more than just polite; it was, I flatter myself, as genuine as applause ever is. Certainly, there was no hint of the muttered boos I had been advised to expect by the festival's perhaps panic-prone organisers, and the mild euphoria I felt was marred only by the fact that nobody laughed, not once, at the cluster of jokes in the text.* There followed a few seconds of microphone-tapping indecision – traditional, in my experience, to these events and even re-assuring to members of the public by its implication that intellectuals are human after all, as prone as they themselves are to stumbling on the twin tripwires of accident and error. Then Jochen proceeded to read, in his own German version, another tale from the collection (at greater length than the original, it seemed to me, but literature does tend to put on

---

* It's curious. I would be downright disbelieving if a reader confessed to me to having laughed out loud at any of my jokes on the printed page, yet it's really quite off-putting when the same jokes, delivered not in print but in person, are met with silence.

weight in translation). A lot of laughter this time and, at the end, warmer applause than there had been for me.

Whereupon he suggested that we immediately move on to the public Q & A session. Now those of my fellow-writers who are reading me will understand what I mean when I say that what invariably occurs at this stage of every such event is that the audience sits there like a pile of Christmas toys for which batteries haven't been included, and it's only after the Q & A has been brought to an abrupt and rather ignominious end, with a wry apology to the visiting author for the congenital bashfulness of the local population, that half of those present make a beeline for the dais to ask all the questions they had been invited to ask during the one part of the evening which had been specifically set aside for their participation. Not, however, on this occasion. No doubt because I faced an assembly of specialists, some of whom were writers themselves, I found myself frantically fielding one question after another like a goalie during a penalty shootout.

We started off with the usual hoary time- and tradition-honoured posers.* 'Mr Adar [sic], where do you get your ideas from?' Me: 'From the dictionary.' 'What, if you please, is your definition of a writer, a real writer?' Me: 'A real writer is one who writes in the first-person-singular even when he doesn't use the word "I".' 'Do you meticulously plot out

* I have included only those questions to which I gave memorable answers.

89

your novels before writing them?' Me: 'Quite the reverse. I leap from the plane and trust not just that my parachute will open but that I won't land in a tree.' 'Have you ever been tempted to imitate the writings of Grim Grin?' Me (venturing a wild guess): 'Not in the least. However, I do increasingly admire those novels of his which he called "entertainments".' 'You wrote two pastiches of Agatha Christie, *The Act of Roger Murgatroyd* and *A Mysterious Affair of Style*? Will there be a third?' Me: 'Absolutely not. I have had my fill of cardboard characters and preposterous plotlines. What I desire to write now is something more personal, a work of genuine depth and ambition.' A comment that prompted an embarrassingly audible, head-turning snort from the back of the hall. Then a (planted) question from Düttmann: 'What is the difference between bookshops in Switzerland and bookshops in Britain?' Me (not impromptu): 'Your bookshops sell fifty types of books and one type of coffee, while ours sell fifty types of coffee and one type of book.' Which instantly provoked an unplanted query from Hugh Spaulding: 'What type?' Me: 'Lite-lit.' Adding (impromptu): 'What you might call skinny litte.' (Some chuckles, but only from the small contingent of real Anglophones.)

Several more questions followed in the same unthreatening vein before we got down to cases. A bearded young man sitting in the centre of the front row having disserted at extravagant length on the sociology of those 'relevant' modern thrillers whose guilty party, whose least likely suspect, or most likely suspect, is infallibly revealed to be society itself, I answered, when he finally let me speak, 'Relevance I can get at home.' (It got the biggest laugh of the evening.) A hand at the back waved an illustrated programme: 'You were not of course the first to do it, not by a long chalk, but may we know what made you write a collection of apocryphal Sherlock Holmes stories?' Me: 'Interesting you should ask that. As it happens, it was a consequence of my rereading the entire Holmes canon in the stupendously annotated edition by Leslie Klinger, which I'm certain you all know well. I eventually arrived at the first of the "posthumous" volumes, *The Return of Sherlock Holmes*, after Conan Doyle had rashly tried to kill off his creation, his Frankenstein's monster, you might say, by having him tumble over the Reichenbach Falls, and I had just begun reading its opening story, "The Mystery of the Empty House", when – well, ladies and gentlemen, you can imagine the surprise and pleasure I experienced on discovering – on rediscovering after a great many years – that the victim of that first murder mystery to be investigated by the Great Detective in the wake of his resurrection was the Honourable Ronald . . . *Adair*. That for me was, as we British say, the clincher.' (Somebody applauded, probably Düttmann.)

Now came one of the warned-of anorak-y questions. 'Mr Adair, in the story you just read to us, Sherlock Holmes, Dr Watson and Dr Eustace Gable travel to Aylesbury by the

8.15 train from the station of King's Cross. I have to tell you this is not possible.' Me: 'Why not?' 'If you wished to travel from London to Aylesbury in the early years of the twentieth century, you must take a train from Marylebone, Paddington or Euston station, never King's Cross.' Me: 'Thank you. I'll make sure that is corrected in the second edition. If there is a second edition.' From Sanary, who alone stood up to ask his question: 'Why cannot you create your own detective instead of stealing somebody else's?' Me: 'As a writer I've always been a shameless poacher of idiolects. As such I've never sought to conceal from the reader the referential mode, nor even the specific literary template, of any of my novels. Lewis Carroll, James Barrie, Jean Cocteau, Thomas Mann, Henry James, Alfred Hitchcock, a plump cinematic cuckoo in the literary nest, these among other more peripheral inspirers have furnished successive models for my published fiction. I read a book, *Alice in Wonderland*, *Peter Pan*, *Les Enfants terribles*, *Death in Venice*, or whatever, I like it, I rewrite it. I am in short a pasticheur. Less by opportunism, though, than by superstition. I long ago discovered that I could embark on a new work of fiction only if its premise had already been legitimised by one of the writers in my personal Pantheon. Each of my novels is thus a palimpsest. Scrape away at its surface and you will find, underneath, another novel, usually a classic. I offer no apology for this.'

Then just as Jochen, I could sense, was about to wrap up the proceedings, a female voice roared out from the very last row, a voice I found unsettlingly familiar even if for the moment I could put neither a face nor a name to it. Her question: 'In "The Giant Rat of Sumatra" you have Holmes express a preference for what he calls "minor oddities" over "major monstrosities". Yes?' Me (suddenly all goose-pimply): 'Yes . . .?' 'And when he draws his finger along the floorboard and holds it up for inspection, and Watson protests that he cannot see anything, Holmes answers – and a very Holmesian answer it is too, I may say – "That is the minor oddity." I'm not misquoting you, am I?' Me: 'No, you aren't.' 'Well then, I'd like you to explain why you employed precisely – and I mean *precisely* – that same conceit of the absence of dust considered as a minor oddity, and in an attic to boot, in the first of your two Agatha Christie pastiches, *The Act of Roger Murgatroyd*. Also, while I've got the floor,' she went on, 'is there any special reason why Dr Gable shares the same Christian name with one of the main characters in both *The Act of Roger Murgatroyd* and *A Mysterious Affair of Style*, my very dear Eustace Trubshawe, former Chief-Inspector of Scotland Yard?'

My very dear Eustace Trubshawe?

'I'm sorry, Miss . . . Miss . . .?'

She rose to her feet. That tricorne hat! Those pince-nez! That garish two-piece suit! Evadne Mount, as I lived and breathed!

I was speechless. By that I mean, I had no speech prepared. Even if it hadn't been she who posed the question, I doubt I could have offered a satisfactory response to it, since until that very instant I hadn't realised I'd actually done what she'd accused me of doing. Yet the instant her accusations were aired, I knew them to be true. (Mortified as I was, however, I remained rational enough not to try mentally passing the buck, blaming my editor, my proof-reader, anybody but myself, for not having picked up on my self-plagiarism. Since I had failed to catch it, why should I have expected them to?) Mumbling some triteness about Homer nodding, I let a puzzled Jochen call the whole event to a decidedly anti-climactic close.

And now I must beg the reader's indulgence with an unavoidable digression.

If by chance you've read those two Agatha Christie parodies-*cum*-celebrations-*cum*-critiques of mine which are alluded to above, you will recall that the first is set in the nineteen-thirties and the second a decade later, just after the Second World War. Also that, aided and abetted by her loyal, long-suffering partner-in-detection, ex-Chief-Inspector Eustace Trubshawe, the same amateur sleuth, Evadne Mount, author of innumerable bestselling mystery novels and the bastard offspring of Christie herself and her own fictional alter ego, the whodunit-writing, apple-munching Ariadne Oliver, presides over both. You will also recall that, just as Hercule Poirot never (or almost never) aged from his first to his last recorded case, from *The Mysterious Affair at Styles*, published in 1920, to *Curtain*, published in 1975, so neither

Evadne nor Eustace, meeting up in the Ritz tearoom in the opening chapter of *A Mysterious Affair of Style,* looks a day older to the other than when they had joined forces to solve the Roger Murgatroyd case a decade earlier. That, of course, was a conscious ploy on my part. I had fun with the cliché and I hoped the reader would too.

Considering, then, what I've just written, it would be perfectly understandable if the same reader, re-encountering Evadne Mount in this memoir, were to shrug off as more postmodern high jinks, as yet another playful subversion of the genre's conventions, the apparent implication that the woman must now be pushing a hundred-and twenty. No need! The Evadne Mount I stared at across a crammed lecture hall in the Meiringen Kunsthalle was just a month or two short of her sixty-sixth birthday.

How come? The story started three years ago at the West London home of the writer and publisher Carmen Callil. We were lounging in the garden before dinner, we being Marina Warner, essayist and polymath; Jules and Pat, i.e. the novelist Julian Barnes and his wife, the literary agent Pat Kavanagh; actor and man-about-town Peter Eyre; and, of course, irrepressible Carmen herself. Somebody – it was Marina, I think – had just asked me whether I had any current project and I replied that I rather fancied writing a parody of vintage Agatha Christie, a novel in black-and-white, as it were, like one of those feebly directed but sparklingly scripted and gloriously well-acted prewar British films

which are for me one of the definitions of sheer, uncompli-
cated bliss, but that I hadn't yet hit upon the iconographical
trappings, both gestural and sartorial, of my cardboard
cutout of a sleuth. Spearing one of her own cocktail
sausages, Carmen said:

'You know, darling, I may just be able to help you there.'

'Oh. How so?'

'Well . . . as it turns out, I'm personally acquainted with a
parody, a living parody, of Agatha Christie.'

'What *do* you mean, Carmen?'

'I mean my friend Evadne Mount.'

'Evadne Mount?' I said, savouring the two strangely plea-
surable words on my tongue. 'I do like the name, but I can't
say it rings any bells for me.'

'I didn't think it would,' she replied. 'She doesn't write the
kind of books someone like you would ever condescend to
read. Except,' she spoke again after a short pause, 'if you
really are planning to do a Christie sort of thingie . . .'

'Do stop teasing, Carmen,' I said impatiently. 'Why do
you think she might interest me? It could be important.'

First asking around if anybody's glass needed topping up,
but everybody was fine, then commanding me to follow her
back into the kitchen, where she had to oversee the roast,
she told me about her friend.

Their first encounter had been at the literary festival in
Hay-on-Wye, to which they had both been invited to debate
the topic 'Feminism or Femininity?'. In spite of the fact that

Evadne's novels – or Evie's, as I now feel more comfortable referring to her – were not really Carmen's thing, they had taken an instant liking to one another and had begun to meet regularly for high tea at one of the posher Piccadilly tearooms. As for those novels, it seems that they were all conscious retreads of the cosy whodunits of the Golden Age of English crime fiction, Agatha Christie's in particular, and had been mildly successful – she did have her following – if rather less so in recent years. In fact, said Carmen, Evie's current anxiety was that, as a single lady without close family connections or any sort of private income, if and when she finally slipped off the mid-list (by which I mean those authors whose books sell just enough copies to persuade their publishers to keep on bringing them out until one fine day they decide not to), she would probably, and sooner rather than later, end up as a homeless bag lady.

I was as baffled as I was intrigued.

'But what are these novels?' I asked. 'I read whodunits. Why have I never heard of hers?'

'Oh, darling, you have me there. It's been so awfully long since I read any of them myself. There was one, I remember, called *The Hour of 12*. No, no, *The Stroke of 12*. And another two which had kind of a gastronomic theme, *The Proof of the Pudding* and *The Timing of the Stew*. Quite good fun. Except that they weren't really topnotch and it all became hugely embarrassing when Evie began badgering me to publish one of her books as a Virago Modern Classic.'

'Not one of her whodunits?'

'Good Lord, no. Even she knew better than to push her luck that far. No, it was an early effort that she'd had published privately and let go out of print, a bit Lesbian, *The Urinal of Futility*, can you imagine, all very *simpatico* in its way but just too terrible as prose. I mean to say, I know that at Virago we sometimes had to stretch the definition of classic – all in the good cause – but even so, there are limits.'

She started hunting for a spatula which, it turned out, she'd been using as her cookbook's bookmark.

'Well, anyway, as I was saying, it was awkward having to refuse her, in fact it became quite unpleasant, our being friends and everything, but I *was* a publisher, after all, and her work just wasn't up to snuff.'

'And yet you still think I ought to read her?'

'No, no, darling, you've completely misunderstood. I think you ought to *meet* her.'

'Meet her? Why?'

'You'll see.'

'Okay, but when?'

'Soon. I'll have you both to supper. It'll be just the three of us. A *tête-à-tête-à-tête*.'

So it was that, a fortnight later, I did meet Evadne Mount. Moreover, the moment I watched her stride into Carmen's living-room, I knew why the meeting had been set up. Evadne Mount was not merely the author of Agatha

Christieish whodunits, four of which I had in the meantime unearthed from my local library's vaults and read with moderate enjoyment, she herself was a character straight out of their stock barrel. Although the evening was humid, she wore a two-piece, oatmeal-hued outfit in the heaviest and hairiest of Scottish tweeds. Her grey stockings were as thick and tight and unappetising as month-old bandages, and her massive feet were encased in the kind of shoes that I would later describe in *The Act of Roger Murgatroyd* as 'so sensible you felt like consulting them on whether you should cash in your shares in Amalgamated Copper'. Then there was that voice of hers with its breaking-the-sound-barrier boom, a voice to whose uniqueness, in neither of the whodunits in which I cast her as my heroine, would I prove capable of doing justice. In truth, if I had been a totally free agent, and hadn't had to worry about her own personal reaction once the books were published, I would have written about it, vulgarly but honestly, that it made her sound as though she were farting through a trumpet.

Somewhat to my surprise, though, I too liked her. We at once struck up a rapport. Even if, as soon as we had been introduced, she started calling me by my first name, standing on the absence of ceremony, so to speak, a liberty I myself never take with strangers, I found that on an unexpectedly wide range of conversational subject-matter – the superiority of Mayhem Parva mysteries to anything of the sort written nowadays, the increasing omnipresence of weirdos and deadbeats in what were once respectable residential areas of London, the charlatanism of almost all contemporary art – our views converged.

While listening to her hold forth, I soon came to the realisation that, as Carmen had foreseen, I definitely could use her as source material for the leading character of my projected whodunit. I even wondered whether it might be possible not merely to *adapt* her but, in a literal sense, to *adopt* her – in short, *to have Evie herself be my sleuth*. Her name, her clothes, the fact that she herself wrote whodunits in a nineteen-thirties style, were just too perfect, for the nostalgist of English eccentricity that I am, to be compromised by the fiction writer's traditional scruples in such matters (though I was already starting to fantasise how I might actually enhance the anachronistic appeal of those clothes with an accessory that would be distinctive to her, a handbag or a hat, yes, a hat, perhaps a French matelot's tricorne). Her voice, her galumphing mannerisms, above all her habit, when she, Carmen and I began dishing the latest dirt on the denizens (Evie's word) of London's literary scene, of being perpetually reminded of incidents out of her own novels, just as Jane Marple would invoke the trivia of village rumour and gossip when elucidating the ostensibly more recondite set of motivations which lay behind some diabolical metropolitan crime – no, there was no reason at all, it seemed to me, why I couldn't transpose her, intact, into my own whodunit. Dare I ask her if she would consent to become the model for my fictional sleuth? Would she be offended? She herself was not too wellknown and, if Carmen was to be believed, financially insecure. Naturally, I would be prepared to offer her a decent percentage of my novel's advance fee and royalties – 25%, say – no, maybe 20% – plenty of time to work out the details. Moreover, if the book turned out to be the success I hoped it would be, it could well re-boot her own languishing career. What had either she or I to lose?

I put my proposition to her. She heard me out, calmly and attentively; the sole sign of what I read as growing enthusiasm on her part was some fidgety play with her pince-nez. It would be my intention, I explained, to name my sleuth 'Evadne Mount'. I would draw inspiration from her facial features, her gestures and clothing, her entire external appearance. I would allow her character to interrupt the storyline at regular intervals with brief little digests of her own whodunits (whose resident amateur detective, Alexis Baddeley, was also an elderly spinster), some of which, those whose twists I'd refrain from divulging, would indeed be her own, others, those whose twists I *would* divulge, I'd devise myself, subject to her approval. Finally, I would give her a Watson in the guise of a archetypally plodding Scotland Yard Inspector yet would also guarantee that it was she not he who solved the crime.

All this, I say, I pitched without any more input from her than a repeated twiddling of her pince-nez and a twitch of an eyebrow when, just once, she exchanged a bemused glance with Carmen. Then, when I had fallen silent, prior to saying either yes or no she made two requests.

'Will I,' she asked, 'have the right to expropriate those apocryphal plot digests you mention and develop them as full-length plots for any subsequent whodunits I myself might decide to write?'

That request I hadn't expected. But, even though a trifle wary and making a mental note to consult my agent, I saw no pressing reason not to grant it and, as I told myself, there would be nothing to prevent me from later changing my mind.

Then: 'Will I have an absolute veto over anything I take exception to in your description of my appearance or the dialogue you attribute to me?'

'Ah well, no,' I answered firmly. 'No absolute right of veto, I'm afraid. I will, of course, let you read in advance everything in the book relating to you, which, as just about everything in the book *will* relate to you, basically means that I'll be showing you the typescript even before my Faber editor sees it. And I will, as I say, subject all of it to your approval, said approval not to be unreasonably withheld, pardon my legalese. But the final decision as to what does or does not go into my novel must rest with me. Being a novelist yourself,' I craftily added, 'you ought to understand why that has to be.'

Turning to Carmen, she said, 'Tell me what you think.'

'Darling, you can't possibly expect me to advise you on something so unheard-of. How would I know how to calculate the risks involved? The ramifications? All I will say is that I've known Gilbert for many years and I promise you he's to be trusted. Not for a single moment would he – Actually,' she ebulliently interrupted herself, 'what the hell! I will advise you. Go for it, Evie!'

And she did, opining (yes, like one of her own clichéd creations, she actually did opine) that since, whichever decision she took, it was bound to be a mistake, the essential was to make the right mistake, not the wrong one.

Our gentleman's agreement was sealed with an old-fashioned handshake and an ice-cold bottle of Veuve Clicquot that I suspect Carmen had been keeping in readiness for just such an outcome. And since I already knew what the title of my whodunit would be, I raised my glass and proposed a toast:

'To *The Act of Roger Murgatroyd*.'

Up to a point, I stuck to my half of the bargain. A written contract, which we both signed without a qualm, followed our supper together and I dutifully emailed Evie, at evadne-mount@yahoo.co.uk, each chapter as I completed it. I made all of the relatively few minor amendments she insisted upon, mainly having to do with references to her weight but once or twice relating to lines of dialogue she felt were inappropriate to both her factual and fictional selves. She also emailed me in her turn a handful of conceits, most of which

I ignored but one I was happy to use, and not simply in compensation for those I wasn't, that of giving her character the catch-phrase 'Great Scott Moncrieff!'.

Unfortunately for her, though, which is why I prefixed the preceding paragraph with the qualifier 'up to a point', I am less of a writer than, supremely, a rewriter. Writing, I contend, makes a book possible; only rewriting is capable of making it good. For three months after I had delivered my text to Faber, I tirelessly polished it, a process, as ever with me, primarily of excision, ellipsis and elimination, of paring, cropping, thinning out, trimming off and cutting away. But I also seized the opportunity to develop certain internal relationships necessary to what I shall grandly call the narrative's combinatoric structure.*

One of these relationships, inspired by Carmen's revelation of Evie's long unobtainable and apparently unreadable Lesbian apologia, *The Urinal of Futility*, involved Evie herself and the stage and screen star Cora Rutherford. Cora was an invented character, of course, named after the actress Margaret Rutherford who (to Agatha Christie's private vexation) had been hopelessly miscast as Miss Marple in a cycle of film adaptations from the sixties. And, in my revised storyline, she – Cora, that is, not Margaret Rutherford – and Evie were described as having once, during their carefree youth, shared 'a small cold flat and a big warm bed in

---

* Like a roller-coaster, even an 'entertainment', as *The Act of Roger Murgatroyd* was subtitled, needs a solid foundation.

Bloomsbury', before maturing, in Evie's case, into self-elected spinsterdom and, in Cora's, into serial heterosexual monogamy.

It wouldn't exactly be fair to say that I never had any intention of letting Evie, as agreed, vet these late additions. But time pressed, Faber fretted, the printers clamoured, as printers have immemorially done, for the typescript, and my fear was that, if she were to take umbrage and actually demand that I edit them out again, the book's pre-Christmas publication date, so crucial to its Boxing Day setting, would be compromised. So I never did email them to her. (It happens.)

The book written, our correspondence ceased altogether. Which also meant that, as the date of publication loomed, I was assailed by a sentiment of foreboding that few writers of fiction can ever have known: would Evie take exception to the very novel of which she was the principal character? I actually asked myself whether she would go as far as to injunct the book, whatever that precisely entailed. Or whether she could.

That November *The Act of Roger Murgatroyd* came out in Britain to wonderful reviews and pretty good sales. Three months previously, in the late summer, Jochen's translation, *Mord auf ffolkes Manor,* had been published in Germany, where it became a modest bestseller, never ascending to the top of the top-ten thermometer but for several weeks hovering satisfactorily around sixth or seventh place. Meanwhile, a pair of complimentary copies, both inscribed by me, were dispatched to Evie's address in Chelsea.

Then nothing. There came no response of any kind. No call, no letter, no email and, needless to say, no legal proceedings either. Evie appeared not to have tried exploiting the success of my book to arrange to have her out-of-print backlist republished. Nor, as she intimated she might, did she ever advise me that it was her intention to borrow one of my counterfeit plotlets to make of it the premise of some new whodunit of her own. To be sure, I might myself have re-opened the lines of communication; yet I was still too nervous to take the initiative of reviving our relationship, such as it had been, and anyway told myself that the ball was in her court. As the weeks passed, my anxieties ebbed without abating altogether.

Delighted with the reception of *The Act of Roger Murgatroyd,* Walter Donohue, my phlegmatic, soft-spoken editor at Faber, then solicited a sequel. Reluctant at first, I finally agreed to write, for a reason which I justified in its dedication, a second Evadne Mount whodunit, *A Mysterious Affair of Style*. This time I didn't once consult her – despite going so far as to have her fictional persona propose marriage to Trubshawe, a narrative development I was especially pleased with, as a twist that had not, like most twists in most whodunits, been preprogrammed into the genre's genes. I could not help thinking, though, that she might have something rather different to say about it. But, again, I heard nothing.

All of which, dear Reader, should explain why, when I saw Evie rise to her feet in the back row of that lecture hall in Meiringen, my feelings were mixed, to put it mildly, to put it very mildly indeed.

Chapter Six

The Q & A over, the room echoed with a communal exha-
lation of breath, followed by leg stretchings, finger-joint
crackings and cigarette-lighter clickings. I inserted my notes
between the pages of the copy from which I had read aloud.
Folding up his own sheaf of notes, Jochen offered me all the
standard reassurances after a public talk of this kind – how
well it had gone, how gratifying were both the number and
quality of the audience's questions. I only half-listened to
him, distracted as I was by the already forming queue of
dedication-seekers anxious for me to inscribe their copies of
Die unveröffentlichte Fallsammlung von Sherlock Holmes
and other, earlier translated books of mine which had absolutely nothing to do with what Nabokov somewhere
describes as 'a hawk-nosed, lanky, rather likeable private
detective' and weren't, many of them, even mystery novels.
(But one learns not to be picky in these matters. A book sold
is a royalty earned.) I was also distracted by my attempts to
ascertain what Evie was up to. My field of vision was

obscured by diversionary activity, however, and I failed to spot her.

The last of my courtiers having borne off her inscribed copy – 'To Hildegard With Best Wishes From Gilbert Adair' – I was finally free to accept a Gauloise from Jochen and a glass of white wine from one of three circulating trays. And there, all of a sudden, she was. Elbowing a path through my fellow writers – I saw Sanary glare at her as his own glass, one he happened to be holding up to the light, was all but knocked out of his hand – she waddled towards me in her crimson suit, for all the world like the Red Queen, twirling her trademark tricorne hat around a chubby forefinger. But wait, hadn't that hat been one of my inventions? I tried to remember if she had been wearing it at Carmen's dinner party. Or had she since decided to adopt a few of the manners and mannerisms which I had given her namesake in my book? But she was almost upon me now, so I stepped down off the dais and walked forward to meet her.

'Holy Rwanda!' she exclaimed. 'Or would you prefer "Great Scott Moncrieff!"?'

I laughed lightly. We shook hands, and I continued to hold hers in mine.

'Evie! Evie, Evie, Evie. I cannot tell you how glad I am to see you. But why didn't you let me know you were attending the Festival? Or are you by any chance,' I asked, 'the famous Mystery Guest?'

'Me?' she boomed out, just as I had always had her do in my books, again causing heads to turn, and it instantly dawned on me that the snort I had heard during the Q & A must have been hers. 'I'm not nearly famous, or mysterious, enough. No, my coming here was one of those last-minute decisions. I arrived just in time to be too late, ha ha! Arrived this very afternoon, as a matter of fact. I missed the opening gala, missed all the speeches, missed practically everything, except of course your reading. As you can imagine, Gilbert, yours was one event I was determined not to miss.'

Now what, I wondered, did she mean by that? Was she still holding a grudge about my reprehensible failure to contact her after the publication of *The Act of Roger Murgatroyd* and before that of *A Mysterious Affair of Style*? Was this the prelude to our long-awaited and, by me, long-dreaded showdown? Since the air around my discourteous treatment of her would sooner or later have to be cleared, better I take the initiative.

'I say, Evie,' I boldly began, then at once stalled. 'But first tell me *your* news. Are you writing a new book?'

Slyly scrutinising me for a moment or two, she expounded – no, she said:

'I've just finished my latest.'

'Dare I ask what it's about?'

'Why, certainly, my dear. You know me, I've never been coy about my work. It's set in an exclusive boys' public school, the victim is its universally despised Latin master, stabbed through his Adam's apple with the tip of a propelling-pencil, and all the usual suspects are present and correct. Except that not one of those suspects is older than fifteen and the murderer himself turns out to be, in accordance with the Detection Club rule that he or she should always be the least likely, the littlest of them all, an evil rosy-cheeked eight-year-old. I'm thinking of calling it *Eeny-Meeny-Murder-Mo*, a title I've stolen from your *Mysterious Affair of Style*. I trust you have no objection?'

I winced. The moment of truth could no longer be delayed. If I tried changing the subject a second time, I would be twice the coward I already felt myself to be. I had irrationally convinced myself that, just so long as Evie never actually enunciated the title of that second whodunit of mine, there was a chance, a vanishingly small chance, to be sure, but one worth taking nevertheless, that she was ignorant of its existence. Since she clearly was anything but, I would have to bite the bullet.

'Evie,' I began again, 'I think it's time we talked.'

'About what?' she said.

'About *A Mysterious Affair of Style*.'

'Oh yes?'

'Yes. It was unforgivably rude of me not to get in touch with you when it came out. What am I saying? Even before it came out. I ought to have been in contact with you when I was actually writing the thing. Can I assume you did nevertheless receive your percentage of the advance and royalties?'

'Yes, I did. For which, many thanks.'

'Well, I'm pleased to hear that. Yet the truth is that I had not only a financial but a moral obligation towards you. And there, I acknowledge, I let you down miserably.'

'My dear Gilbert, there's no need for you to –'

'Let me finish, please. I took liberties with your image without consulting you first, as I was obliged, contractually obliged, to do. I insist I was as careful as I could be. I trust you noticed, for example, that not one of the casual racist and anti-Semitic gibes that pepper the two books, just as they do Agatha Christie's, was spouted by your character. But it's quite true, I should have obtained your authorisation to write a sequel to *The Act of Roger Murgatroyd*, and I didn't. And then, in *A Mysterious Affair*, my having you wager Trubshawe that you'd solve the crime before he did and, if he lost the bet, his having to marry you –'

'Ah yes, Trubshawe,' she interrupted me with a heavy sigh. 'My darling Eustace.'

'That too was unforgivable. Yet I wouldn't want you to think it was because I was afraid you might object. Naturally, if you *had* objected, I'd have scrubbed it without a second thought. I simply didn't ring you up, don't ask me why, when the idea popped into my head and, once I had actually written the chapter, well, I suppose I genuinely assumed you'd be tickled by it.'

'Oh, I was, I was. Tickled pink,' she replied. 'Why shouldn't Eustace and I have tied the knot? Ours was a marriage made in heaven. Pardon the clitch.'

'Clitch?'

'Cliché, Gilbert, cliché. One of those nasty things you never stop putting in my mouth.'

'*Touché* – or, rather, tootch,' I answered with a rueful smile that brought a grin to her pasty features.

'No,' she said, 'I wasn't affronted by your matchmaking. The less so as it all worked out most satisfactorily. However,' she went on blithely, as I tried to figure out what she meant by 'worked out most satisfactorily', 'however, I do have a bone to pick with you. A bonelet, really.'

I waited in a state of mute apprehension to hear what she was about to come out with now.

First, she noisily cleared her throat. Then:

'As you of all people must know, I'm a very private person. I'm not prone to making public knowledge of any distressed state I might be in, except on that one occasion, of course, with Eustace in the Ritz bar when I owned up to my loneliness. But no – no, I *was* hurt, genuinely hurt.'

'By something I did?'

'Yes, Gilbert, by something you did.'

'Well, but what?' I asked.

'If you must know, I was hurt by *The Unpublished Case-Book of Sherlock Holmes*.'

Delaying a moment or two before answering, I let run

through my mind a few of the reasons she might conceivably have had for being hurt, for God's sake, by this new book of mine, but I couldn't find a single plausible one and finally said:

'I'm sorry, Evie, you really have lost me. If I thought you didn't like the book, well, naturally I'd be disappointed, but, after all, it's a risk every writer faces even with his closest friends. And, to be perfectly frank with you, I flatter myself I'm much less susceptible to criticism than most. It's – well, take this scarf of mine.* If you told me you didn't like it, my response would be that I was sorry but that I didn't buy it to please you. And it's the same with my books.'

'Your scarf I do like. Armani, isn't it?' She fingered it, tentatively twisting it sideways to check the label. 'I'm right, as usual. Matter of fact, I like the scarf quite a lot more than the book.'

'Ah . . .'

'It isn't so much the tome itself, you understand,' she said, adjusting her pince-nez, 'as what you might call its ilk.'

As what *I* might call 'its ilk'?!! There are words, and 'tome' and 'ilk' are two of them, that for me instantly disqualify a writer from serious consideration. No matter. Let's hear what she has to say.

'What's wrong with the ilk?'

'An anthology of apocryphal Sherlock Holmes stories? Such a cheap commonplace idea. You realise that bookshops

---

* I always wear a scarf. It's an indispensable element of my 'look'.

are swarming with them these days? Sherlock Holmes and Jack the Ripper. Sherlock Holmes and Sigmund Freud. Sherlock Holmes and Mata Hari. All of them tosh. I call him – the bogus Holmes – *Schlock* Holmes, ha ha! And, I must say, Gilbert, I would have expected something more original of you, even when you're wearing your pasticheur's hat.'

'That's all very well, Evie,' I replied coldly, 'and insisting as I do that I know better than anybody, friend or critic alike, what the defects of my books are, I honestly don't mind that you didn't care for it. But you still haven't explained why you were hurt.'

There being no ashtray within immediate reach, I let my cigarette butt drop to the floor, as I had already noticed several others doing, and stubbed it out under my shoe.

Evie glanced down at the squashed butt with deep disapproval etched on her countenance – I mean, she looked at it disapprovingly – and said, 'You know, Gilbert, leaving a cigarette end on somebody else's floor is like using somebody else's loo and not flushing the toilet.'

Now I myself flushed. Without bothering to explain that I was merely following a precedent, I picked up the offending little number-two and stuck it into my trouser pocket.

'Well,' I asked again, 'are you going to tell me what it was that hurt you?'

'Haven't you guessed? It's the fact that you wrote two ingenious whodunits of which I was the heroine, they were marketed by Faber as the first two parts of a trilogy and yet, for a reason of your own that I cannot begin to fathom, you elected not to write a third. You dropped me flat without so much as a by-your-leave. And for what, I ask you? A pastiche of Conan Doyle. As though the world needed another.'

To my surprise, I was touched by her admission.

'Evie,' I said, not quite, damn it, striking the half-tender, half-ironic tone I was aiming for, 'if I didn't know you better, I'd say you were jealous.'

'Please don't insult me,' she peevishly replied, 'by calling me jealous. Eustace once tried pulling that stunt and got what-for for his pains. I used the word "hurt", and "hurt" is as far as I'm prepared to go. I was hurt because, without warning, without warning *me*, you cut short a series of whodunits that were already critical and commercial successes. Why, Gilbert, why? I really don't understand.'

I answered in a measured voice that, if I'd done so, it was for a strictly aesthetic reason. For all my efforts to have the second novel ring as many changes on the first as was organically feasible within the generic conventions I was pastiching, there remained a stubbornly samey something about *A Mysterious Affair of Style* which long afterwards nagged at me. And not only at me. One reviewer, praising the book, had also expressed disappointment that I had taken an 'if-it-ain't-broke-don't-fix-it' attitude to the first of the cycle, and I couldn't help agreeing with him.

'For me,' I said, 'another mark of a real writer is that he – or she – fixes things which aren't broken.'

'How very aphoristic of you. But I must tell you, Gilbert, even if *you* cannot, I myself can envisage many new adventures for my namesake to solve, and just as many variations on Agatha's titles, and I give you advance warning that I shan't quit this town before I've persuaded you to come around to my way of thinking.'

This was beginning to sound faintly alarming. I have never read a word of Stephen King, but I once saw a goodish film version of one of his thrillers, *Misery*, about a writer writhing helplessly in the castrating clutches of his most devoted fan, and I knew how he felt. I needed rescuing before Evie's discourse took an even more sinister turn. Peering over at my fellow writers, who were still tribally closeted together, I succeeded in catching Sanary's eye. Desperately but discreetly, I trained a 'For Christ's sake, get me out of this' face on him; and, after a few agonising moments when he did no more than return my look of beseechment with one of bland bemusement, he finally, indolently disengaged himself and came across to join us.

'Oh, there you are,' he said as convivially as he ever managed to say anything to me. 'Looking for you. Wanted to congratulate you. Excellent performance. Some sharp oneliners. Wasted on that audience, though. Except that I did notice you making a scribbled note after each of your zingers. Do I assume that to mean you were mentally filing them away for subsequent recycling? Wise man. For the writer, nothing counts but print.'

'Oh, I don't know,' I murmured. 'Nowadays . . . the Internet . . . all those blogs . . .'

'Nothing to do with us,' he said. 'The Internet is an infinite library of goggle-eyed, Google-eyed ignorance and stupidity. If you don't believe me, Google Tolstoy. Google Dostoevsky.'

'Google Gogol,' Evie piped up unexpectedly.

'Indeed, Google Gogol,' Sanary said with a giggle, for the first time giving Evie a once-over of sidelong curiosity. 'Mark my words, the day literature comes to an end, it won't be because nobody writes any longer but because everybody does. Hey, that's not bad either.' And he hurriedly drew a little notepad out of his blazer pocket, extracted a slender silver pencil from its hollow spine and jotted down his off-the-cuff *mot*.

Vaguely indicating Evie, I asked him, 'Do you two know each other?'

'No,' he said, 'I have not had that pleasure.'

'Evadne Mount, Pierre Sanary.'

'Glad to meet you,' she said, extending a hand. 'Any friend of Gilbert's is a friend of mine.'

He gazed into her face for a moment without saying a word, then raised her hand to his own face and, to my amazement, for it wasn't at all his style, brushed his lips against it.

'Evadne Mount!' he squealed. 'Well, sacred blue!'

Now it was my turn to gaze at Sanary. Although I felt still

somewhat put out by Evie, she was in many ways dear to me and, despite those silly retro-affectations of hers, I had heroically refrained from lampooning her in either of my whodunits; or, if I had done so, there could be no mistaking the affectionate intent, could there? Yet here was Sanary already making fun of her, so it seemed, at their first encounter. Or was an oblique compliment being paid to both of us at once?

Evie, for her part, was unfazed by, or possibly unaware of, what was for me his inadmissable levity.

'Why, Monsieur Sanary,' she simpered, 'and just what am I supposed to make of that exclamation?'

'A thousand pardons, Mademoiselle. It was not of my intention to be rude. It is only that I did not know you were here in Meiringen. If I had known it, you may be sure I would have sought you out at once. I am a great admirer of yours – also, *naturellement*, of Alexis Baddeley.'

'You are?'

'*Mais oui* – but yes. I surprise you?'

'You do a bit.'

'Why?'

'Monsieur Sanary, I won't dissemble. I know you by reputation, of course, who does not, but I must make an embarrassing confession. I have never been able to read your books, even in translation, even your one thriller. I'm afraid they're too intellectual, too theoretical, for my little grey cells, as I suspect,' she couldn't resist adding, 'they'd also be for Hercule Poirot's. My own novels are entertainments, you know, designed to while away an agreeable hour or two. Yours – well, yours, by contrast, are so very *cultural*.'

'Poof, Mademoiselle! I too write to entertain. "It is hardly worth writing", as Raymond Queneau once said – or, as his lipogrammatical clone, Raymond Q. Knowall, is quoted as saying, in the e-less-ese of Georges Perec's *La Disparition*, so admirably recreated in equally e-less English-ese as *A Void* by our mutual friend here – "it is hardly worth writing if it is simply as a soporific." Very true, no? As for what you call "culture", whenever I hear that abominable word, I reach for not the pistol but – how you say? – the pinch of the salt.'

This was the limit. Poor Evie, so marinated was she in her own image, an image partly of my doing, she quite failed to realise that she was being mocked. Yet there was no excuse for Sanary's distasteful send-up of her and if, at that moment, the others had not also suddenly joined us, all of them visibly itching to share some exciting new piece of news, I would certainly have taken him to task, tricky as it would have been without hurting Evie's feelings.

The exciting news was the long-awaited arrival in Meiringen of the Mystery Guest. While chatting to Meredith about the Hungarian writer Agota Kristof* (arresting name!), on whom, before returning to the States, she intended to pay a visit in Zurich coupled with a pilgrimage to the tiny cemetery in Clarens, near Montreux, in which Nabokov's

---

* Author of *The Notebook*, *The Proof* and *The Third Lie*, all well worth reading.

remains are interred, Düttmann had received an agitated call on his mobile. Alerted by the queeny desk clerk, whom I imagined all a-quiver, he had at once rushed off to the Sherlock Holmes Hilton. Not, however, before communicating the news to Meredith on condition that she keep it to herself at least until an official announcement had been made to the media: i.e. to the one seedy journalist from the local rag assigned to cover the Festival. Actually, Meredith took so long to overcome her scruples – 'I really don't think I ought to tell you who it is. I mean to say, I had it from Tommy in confidence. There could be consequences . . .' – that, before she eventually blurted out the Mystery Guest's identity, the canny Sanary had already deduced it from not much more than the strange fact that seemingly nobody from the Festival had been warned in advance when he was due to arrive either at the airport or at the hotel itself.

It was (you're ahead of me, Reader) Gustav Slavorigin, who had secretly flown in on a British military plane and made an unscheduled landing on Swiss soil at some hush-hush airfield in the mountains.

Why, I instantly wondered, had Slavorigin accepted the invitation? Had he grown so stir crazy that the prospect of spending forty-eight hours as the guest of honour of an unpretentious but also unprestigious literary festival in the Bernese boondocks struck him as a heaven-sent break from the frustrations of day-in day-out isolation and confinement? Was it, indeed, the event's very third-ratedness which tempted him, as offering him a chance to be fêted as the literary lion he knew himself to be without the concomitant risk of exposure that he would run at some higher-powered do, assuming there even existed such an event in the world of books?* This, for me, was the real mystery of the Mystery Guest.

Intriguingly, when we started comparing notes, we discovered that, with two exceptions, Evie and Hugh Spaulding, we had all had previous encounters with Slavorigin.

As I wrote earlier, he and I had been contemporaries at Edinburgh University. Sanary, for his part, had written a lengthy, controversial article in the *Tribune de Genève*, one later reprinted both in *Libération* and the *New York Review of Books*, laying out side by side half-a-dozen quite lengthy passages from *Wayfarer*, a novel I described in this memoir's Prologue, and half-a-dozen near-identical passages from an obscure Bulgarian novel published in the nineteen-sixties, one little-read but passionately admired by those few who had read it. He also implied that if *Wayfarer*, 'translated into thirty languages' as the blurb of the paperback edition trumpeted, was never published in Sofia, it was not for the reason offered by Slavorigin himself, that he could comfortably write about his native land only if he knew that nobody

_____

* For better or worse, and probably better, we writers have no Cannes Festival of our own, no waterfall of a red carpet cascading down the steps of the Palais, no superstar poets, novelists or essayists, no pulchritudinous chick-lit starlets coyly mislaying their bikini tops on the *plage*.

in it, and in particular his own close relatives, would ever read him, but rather that he was fearful of being caught red-handed in an unforgivable act of plagiarism. Slavorigin threatened to take legal action but, for whatever reason, confined himself in the end to writing a stinging response in, precisely, the *New York Review of Books*. He accused his assailant not only of feigning a fluency in the Bulgarian language which he didn't possess – although, in actual fact, Sanary had made no such pretence, having depended for the nitty-gritty details of his exposé on an acquaintance of his, a Bulgarian-born academic in the Department of Slavic Languages at the University of Basel – but also of professional jealousy born of personal talentlessness. Displaying, in his counter-response, a lofty disregard for Slavorigin's *ad hominem* insults and insinuations, Sanary made the further point that *Wayfarer* wasn't the first occasion on which the Anglo-Bulgarian author had, as he coyly but killingly phrased it, 'cherry-picked another man's brains': *A Sensitive Dependence on Initial Causes* shared its premise of a suicide's last day on earth with *Le feu follet*, a semi-classic novel, conveniently unread beyond the French hexagon, by Pierre Drieu la Rochelle, a dandified *tombeur de dames*, a Nazi collaborationist and an eventual suicide himself. And since these were unlikely to be the last of his thefts, it would be interesting, he concluded menacingly, to know what some more thorough translingual investigation might still uncover.

Meredith had interviewed Slavorigin for the *Paris Review* in the immediate wake of the scandal provoked by *Out of a Clear Blue Sky*. They hadn't got on. She had thought him odious, and near as dammit said so in print, odious above all for his derisive attitude towards September 11. As for Autry, who had met him around the same period, he stated only, without elaborating on its relevance to his view of the man, that he himself had witnessed the fall of both Towers from the twenty-seventh storey window of his publisher's office. Finally, unknown to any of us, including me, it transpired that Jochen had actually been the German translator of Slavorigin's first novel, *Dark Jade*. He, too, had found him a handful. Why, we asked.

'Well, as most writers would, I suppose, he wanted me to translate his novel as literally as possible without doing violence to the language I was translating it into. Naturally, I had no problem with that, and so I rendered the title as *Dunkle Jade*, which in German does mean nothing more than *Dark Jade*. But Slavorigin wasn't satisfied. To his English ear, he told me, *dunkle* was a silly-sounding word. He asked me if it wouldn't remind German readers, as it reminded him, of *dummkopf*. I assured him it wouldn't. He still wasn't satisfied. And he got his way, his pig-headed way. The book was eventually published as *Lust*. What a title! Not to mention that it had already been taken by Elfriede Jelinek. The man may be a genius,' he said calmly, 'he's also a *dummkopf* himself. A fucking buffoon.'

For a writer it always comes as a slight shock to hear his translator pronounce a word he himself has never asked him to translate, especially if it's one of the f-words. There was a silence. Then Evie, who couldn't abide silences, spoke up.

'As somebody once said, fasten your seatbelts, it's going to be a bumpy ride.'

'Sure and begorrah!' exclaimed Hugh. 'That it is!'

I thought my head would burst.

Chapter Seven

The restaurant in which we all dined together that evening,[*] situated six or seven kilometres out of town, was housed inside a pseudo-Palladian pavilion set down in a paradisal, many-acred park. In the dining room itself were more gilt-framed mirrors, ugly ormolu mantelpiece clocks and heavy velveteen curtains than I had ever seen together in any interior. All in all, it was one of those pretentious establishments in which, by a curious paradox, the extortionate prices paid by their clients, prices we could only guess at as the menu gave no indication of what they might be, are also part of what is being paid for.

Sweet and schoolboyish in a sober pinstriped suit which wasn't, but looked at though it were, two sizes too large for him, Düttmann was already there when I arrived just behind Hugh Spaulding, with whom I'd shared the first of a small fleet of laid-on taxis. About a minute into the ten-minute

<hr>

[*] Except for Jochen, who had to fly off to Hamburg, where his presence had been requested at another literary festival the very next day.

ride, Hugh had begun a conversation with me that was still ongoing when our driver pulled up in the pavilion's tree-lined driveway, which meant that we were obliged to continue talking outside in the cold for a while longer before entering. It turned out that he was in grave financial difficulties.

'Gilbert,' he said to me, a pungent aroma of peppermints on his breath, 'I'll come clean right off. You know I'm Irish, etc?'

'Of course.'

'But what you probably didn't know is that I haven't lived in Ireland for the last fifteen years.'

'No, actually I didn't. I suppose I just assumed –'

'The thing is, etc, the taxman didn't know it either.'

'Aha, I see. And now –'

'I know, I know!'

'I'm sorry. You know what?'

'What you're going to say. And you'd be right. The Inland Revenue – the British Inland Revenue, etc – has just found out, etc, etc, that I've been resident in this country – I mean, in England – for fifteen years and now they're chasing me for back taxes, ten years of back taxes.'

'Not fifteen?' I asked maybe a bit callously, but I was distracted by his verbal twitch of tacking 'etc' onto every other phrase.

'Ten's the legal limit, thank God for small mercies.'

'But can't you argue that you already paid Irish taxes?'

'Are you deliberately not getting it, Gilbert?' he answered testily, lighting a cigarette in defiance of the (even if one had no German) manifest 'No Smoking' sign on the glass partition which separated us from the driver. 'You're a writer yourself. Surely you've heard that creative artists like us are exempt from income tax in Ireland. I haven't paid a penny in years.'

'H'm. That's bad.' (I started to have an idea where all of this was leading.)

'Too right it's bad. It's worse than you think.'

'Oh?'

'I haven't got it. The old thrillers, etc, etc, aren't selling so well any more. Last one brought me in £784 in royalties. I used to get twenty times that.'

'I'm really sorry, Hugh. I had no idea you –'

'I know, I know! You thought, once a bestseller, always a bestseller. Well, I tell you, it doesn't always work like that, etc, etc, as you'll discover for yourself one day. No, no, no,' he hastily corrected himself, 'you'll be all right. You're bound to be all right so long as you keep churning out your Agatha Christie imitations. There'll always be readers for stuff like yours, even if it isn't the real McCoy.'

I was about to disabuse him, to inform him that cod-Christiana, especially if it has been produced by a writer to whose reputation the label of postmodernism has been attached, is no infallible recipe for bestsellers, when he bluntly came to the point.

'The thing is, your being an old friend of mine [?], in the same line of business, except you're doing much better than me, I thought you might be able to help me over the hump, etc. As one writer to another, like.'

'How much do you need?' I asked quietly.

'Well . . .' I sensed him manfully squaring up. 'Ten thousand would keep the bastards at bay.'

'Ten thousand? Ten thousand pounds?!'

His face crumpled up like an empty brown paper bag.

'Look, if that's too much, what about seven-and-a-half? Or seven? Even seven would give me a bit of a breathing space.'

The taxi was now parked directly in front of the entrance to the pavilion. We both got out. Puffing, fanning himself with a magazine he must have picked up from the reception desk – the taxi, like everything else in this cold country, had been overheated and his own cigarette smoke hadn't helped – Hugh adroitly barred my way in, treating me to a long and remarkably frank account of how he had frittered away his earnings.

'Well, will you help me out?'

'It's not that I won't, Hugh. I can't.'

I laboriously spelt out to him why not. I cannot claim any originality for my catalogue of excuses, save that they were all true. I told him, for example, that even if my books had done reasonably well, none of them had come close to being a bestseller. That I lived a carelessly unthrifty life myself, basically surviving from one advance to the next. That I had a number of crippling monthly outgoings – because of my Blockley cottage, I paid two sets of utility bills, two council tax bills, etc, etc (as he would say). As for my royalties, fairish as they now tended to be, particularly in Germany, I added, an admission which slightly weakened my case, but demonstrated, as it was intended to, that I wasn't lying to him, don't forget that my agent takes fifteen per cent of them and the taxman thirty to forty per cent of what's left. And, as there was of course a mortgage on my Notting Hill flat, and I was, well, getting on, any loose cash which swum into my ken I had to put aside to reduce that mortgage to a size I could live with, so that even if I did have ten thousand pounds to spare, which I didn't, I couldn't afford to lend it to him.

Well before I finished speaking, he had ceased to listen. Hugh was incorrigibly feckless, to be sure, but he was probably no novice in situations of this kind. After only a few words of mine he would have realised he was out of luck. From his vantage point most of what I had just said was redundant.

'I know, I know! [another tic]' he snapped at me. 'Let's pretend I never asked you.' And he silently turned away and started to mount the steps into the pavilion. After a moment or two I followed him in.

Inside, at the bar, each of us was offered a flute of champagne by a flushed and nervous Düttmann. Hugh swallowed his at one go and grabbed another. I meanwhile asked Düttmann if all the arrangements relating to Slavorigin had proved satisfactory. He fell silent. He asked if I had ever met him. I told him I had and he lapsed into silence again. Then he said:

'Mr Slavorigin is one of the greats, I know. But he has many peculiarities. Magnificent peculiarities, I grant you, but many none the less.'

I bemusedly agreed with him, then took myself off to the Gents. The palms of my hands were sweating, possibly something I had caught from Hugh.

When I returned ten minutes later, Düttmann had been joined by Meredith, ravishing as ever in a jet-black trouser-suit, Evie, Sanary and Autry, though as yet there was no sign of Slavorigin.

Autry, who was wearing a more formal and less sloppy variation of his usual outfit, his inevitable black string tie held in place by a small and surprisingly stylish clip in the shape of a cow's skull, stood facing the rest of the company with his two elbows resting behind him on the bar, all the while shifting a toothpick from one corner of his mouth to the other like some fancy riverboat gambler rotating a coin over, under and around his versatile fingers. From time to time I saw him mutely resist an attempt by Düttmann to have him participate in the discussion in which he,

Düttmann, was engaged with Sanary and Evie. I too chose to sit that one out. I could already overhear Sanary, in his maddening element, lecturing them on the subject of some magnificent peculiarity, to borrow Düttmann's admirable locution, in the movie adaptation of Dashiell Hammett's *The Thin Man* and I was just not in the mood.* I therefore ended up talking to Meredith, who had, she confessed to me, excused herself a minute before from the same discussion, one which held no interest for her.

Our own conversation was playful but still just a wee bit edgy. Meredith had mellowed. Or perhaps our earlier run-in had been no more than a minor casualty of September 11. At any rate, despite a grating tendency on her part to be busier-than-thou – if I told her I was about to start a new book, then so it seemed was she; if I mentioned that the film rights to my *Buenas Noches Buenos Aires* were being negotiated as we spoke, she at once had to let me know that she had just done lunch with an *extremely* hot young Hollywood director, whom she could not possibly name, about

---

* Sanary, strangely, had a voice that was both soft and metallic, even piercing at times, and, although I tried not to eavesdrop, I still couldn't help hearing the essential of this latest bee in his bonnet. In case any reader is curious, it concerned the fact that in Hammett's novel the eponymous thin man is actually the victim, the victim of the murder on which its plot revolves, and not the detective. Hence the titles of the five film sequels which followed the first adaptation itself – *After the Thin Man*, *Another Thin Man*, *Shadow of the Thin Man* and so on – made no sense whatsoever. For once I already knew that.

the eventuality of her being hired as consultant on a big-budget biopic of Sappho for Nicole Kidman – despite that tendency, I found her, shall I say, a lot more than bearable although even now a little less than likeable.

It was, in fact, while I was chatting to her that, over her left shoulder, I saw him. Flanked by two burly, moustachioed goons, obviously his bodyguards, Slavorigin stepped, shakily, I thought, into the bar. Even after all these years he was charisma incarnate. His gleaming white smile was as agreeable to the eye as the orange glow of an unoccupied taxi in the fading light of a rainy afternoon. His long black hair – this I had only ever seen in gossip-column snapshots – was set in stark relief by a single thick white streak which swept across one side of his squarish head like Susan Sontag's or Sergei Diaghilev's (except that in the Russian impresario's case the white, not the black around it, was its natural shade). He had kept his figure enviably trim and wore a super snakeskin jacket, fastidiously baggy denim jeans and brown suede moccasins.

It so chanced that, as he approached our little group, everyone's back but mine was turned to him. Putting a finger to his lips, he gestured at me not to give him away. Without having the faintest notion of what he was up to, I complied. He tiptoed over to Meredith, who, as I say, faced away from him, and to my horror clamped both his hands not on her eyes but on her breasts, from behind, and yelled out:

'Yoo hoo! Guess who!'

She shrieked. Like Cora Rutherford's in the murder scene of *A Mysterious Affair of Style*, the stem of her champagne glass snapped in half. Giving Düttmann such a shove in the small of his back he nearly fell over, the two bodyguards made a simultaneous dash forward, their intention presumably to bundle Slavorigin out of the pavilion into some bullet-proof limousine parked in the driveway. Her face a mask of scrunched-up fury, Meredith meanwhile wheeled around as if to berate then castrate the neanderthal galoot who had practically raped her in public. Yet, the instant she saw who it was, she faltered, shuddered, then uttered the single word, 'Prick!'

Slavorigin, who had yet to acknowledge my presence, treated her to a goatish grin.

'Merry . . . Merry . . .'

'Don't call me Merry, you scumbag!' she cried, while I prudently relieved her of the broken champagne glass.

'But I don't understand,' he went on, now all whiny hurt and puzzlement. 'What happened to the Meredith I knew that night –'

'Shut up!' she shouted so loudly that his minders, who had momentarily scaled back their projected rescue operation, started moving in again.

'Oh, for fuck's sake go away, you revolting little men!' Slavorigin barked, dismissing them with a drunken wave of his long feminine fingers. (I had already noticed the silver screw-top of a flask peeping out of the hip pocket of his jeans.)

With the comical deference of emissaries taking undulatory leave of a monarch, Thomson and Thompson, as I had begun to think of them, slowly, silently backed off, and he turned to face Meredith again.

'That night, that heavenly night, at the Carlyle . . .'

'Will you SHUT UP!'

'What? Where's that famous von Demarest sense of self-disparaging humour?'

'Look, if you don't . . . I'm going to have to leave. Right now. I mean it.'

'Please, please, Miss Demarest,' said Düttmann frantically, 'I'm certain there's no call for –'

'I'm sorry, but I really don't see how I can stay.'

'But you mu–'

'Of course, of course you must stay!' Slavorigin cut in. 'I apologise. I'm not sure why I should, but I do. Sorry, sorry, sorry. But I'd just like to add that you look so unbelievably scrumptious tonight I feel like – All right, all right! I won't say another word. Oh dear. Nobody loves Gustav.'

Then, abruptly, to Düttmann:

'Say, who do you have to fuck to get a drink around here?'

'Oh, but the drinks are free of charge.'

Slavorigin smiled, a lovely melting smile, I do admit.

'You're adorable. Everybody's adorable. Everybody but me. I'm a rotter. Well, Tommy,' he said, squeezing Düttmann's hand as it proffered him a glass of champagne, 'aren't you going to introduce me to your friends?'

'Of course. I think' – poor Düttmann looked helplessly in my direction – 'I think you already know Gilbert Adair.'

'Ah, Gilbert.' Slavorigin smiled at me with the phony raffish bonhomie I remembered of old. 'How *are* you? God, don't you ever age? To tell you the truth, I've thought a lot about you these past two years.'

This was news to me.

'You have?'

'In captivity, you see' – he sniggered – 'makes me sound like a panda – in captivity I live on a diet of thrillers. I waded through Agatha Christie – hadn't looked at them since I was a boy – and when I'd read all of hers, well, naturally, like most of your readers, I guess, I had to make do with yours. Clever contraptions, both of them. You really caught the cardboard quality of her characters. Anyway, they helped pass the time.'

'Thank you.'

'Got good reviews, too, I noticed. Deserved to.'

'Thanks again.'

'Also a couple of stinkers.'

'Just one, I think. In the *Guardian*. Michael Dibdin.'

'Who died not long afterwards. *Spooooky* . . . Still, I do seem to recall there was another. In one of the Sundays. No?'

'No.'

A silence followed this ersatz jocularity, Düttmann uncertain whether or not he should proceed with the introductions. Observing him with amusement, Slavorigin said:

'Pinter should be here.'

'You mean,' said Düttmann tentatively, 'he would make the party go with a swing?'

Both Slavorigin and I burst into loud laughter. He gently caressed Düttmann's blush-red cheek.

'You know, you really are adorable. Where have you been all my life?'

'In Meiringen,' was Düttmann's naive and winning reply.

Slavorigin laughed again.

'What I meant, Tommy my darling, was that Pinter should be here with a notepad, taking down all these pregnant pauses.'

'Ah.'

'But go on, do your hostess thing. Present me to the other guests.'

Düttmann introduced Slavorigin first to Autry, who shook hands with him but did not speak, continuing instead to transfer his toothpick from one side of his insolent mouth to the other. Then to Hugh, whose thrillers Slavorigin claimed, like Sanary, and all very extraordinarily to me, to have read and enjoyed, and he might well have done, as he cited the title of one of them, *Murder Under Par*, of whose existence I was unaware. A beaming Hugh suggested that they have 'a private little *conversazione* together', to which Slavorigin, restless eyes already elsewhere, answered, 'Absolutely!'

The next introduction was to Sanary, which engendered this exchange:

DUTTMANN [*to Slavorigin*]: May I present Pierre Sanary?
SANARY [*extending a hand*]: How do you do?
SLAVORIGIN [*shaking it*]: I'm very well, thank you. You?
SANARY [*withdrawing his hand*]: I have nothing to complain of.
SLAVORIGIN [*withdrawing his*]: Good.
DUTTMANN [*to Slavorigin with perceptible relief*]: Last but not least, I'd like you to meet an uninvited but nevertheless welcome guest of our Festival, Evadne Mount.
EVIE [*coyly rebuking him*]: Actually, it's Evadne Trubshawe.

'Dame Evadne Mount!' Slavorigin cried. 'Well, well, well! You're one of my heroines.'

'How very nice of you to say so,' she answered with the simper she seemed to hold in reserve exclusively for compliments. 'But I'm not a Dame yet, you know.'

'Any day now, dear lady, any day now. I cannot tell you with what interest I've followed your career. Criminology, you know, is my hobby, my *violin d'Ingres*, as the French say. And I was supine, simply *supine*, with admiration for the brilliance with which you solved that dastardly crime at ffolkes Manor. Even better, the poisoning of poor Cora Rutherford at – Ealing, was it?'

'Elstree.'

'Elstree, of course. Your reasoning – ah!' Pinching a hollow moue with the tips of his thumb and index finger, he bestowed on them both a big slurpy kiss. 'Mmmph, what a masterpiece! Only you could have deduced a murderer's identity from the style of his film. If ever I decide to write a whodunit, I may well ask you to let me use that case as its plot. All names changed, of course.'

'Always happy to oblige, Mr Slavorigin.'

'Gustav, call me Gustav. Or Gussie,' he added with a flourish of his forelock, and I couldn't help noticing that, the longer he talked to Evie, the swishier he became. 'Not Gus, you understand, no, no, I won't have Gus. But Gussie's nice. Like Gussie Moran, whoever she was. But what was I saying?' he mumbled, his eyes straining to focus on Evie. 'Oh yes, Cora Rutherford. I must tell you, Evadne – may I call you Evadne? – your success in bringing her murderer to book was *soooh* important to me. I was a very great admirer of Cora Rutherford.'

'Were you?' exclaimed Evie. 'Ah, but I don't suppose you ever saw her on stage? I always say that nobody who saw her only on the films knew the real Cora.'

'How right you are. But the fact is, I did. I did see her on stage. Just once, when I was a boy, a mere slip of a boy. In *Private Lives*.'

He turned to me. 'It's a play by Noël Coward.' Then he returned to Evie.

'She was *divine*. Of course, if I put a gun at my own back and compel myself to be brutally honest, she was also a teensy-weensy bit too old for the part. Yet she had such star quality, you know, she made everybody else look too young. But what am I thinking of?'

He slipped his hand inside his snakeskin jacket and pulled out an exquisite *art déco* wallet in pale grey suede. From inside that he took a squared-off wad of folded-up newspaper which he then unfolded in front of us.

'Her performance was such a formative revelation for me,' he said, holding up a wrinkled page of newsprint, 'that I clipped this ad out of the paper and I've worn it next to my heart ever since.'

Craning to see for myself, I felt as if I had just had a glistening ice cube forced down my throat. There it was, yellowing but still perfectly legible, an advertisement for the Apollo Theatre, Shaftesbury Avenue: 'Rex Harrison and Cora Rutherford in Noël Coward's *Private Lives*. Second Record-Breaking Year!' And that second record-breaking year into the play's run was 1958.

I was, to use one of my favourite words, discombobulated. I must give this one, I said to myself, serious thought. Considering that Slavorigin was born in 1955, it meant that he would have been taken to see Coward's brittle little trifle at the age of three, which, preposterous as that notion already was, couldn't in any case have been true since, at least according to his many profiles, interviews, *A Biography of Myself*, etc, when his family quit Sofia to resettle in London, he himself was four years old. So he definitely did not watch Cora Rutherford performing on stage in 1958! Whereupon, just as I was mentally adding that lie to the ever-expanding inventory of his well-established economies with the facts of his own life, I also mentally slapped my hand on my brow when it occurred to me that, by 1958, Cora Rutherford had lain twelve years in her grave in Highgate Cemetery, having been murdered on the set of *If Ever They Find Me Dead,* a film shot at Elstree *circa* 1945 or 1946. Another lie, to which – but, wait, am I crazy or what? Cora was a *fictional* character – a character invented *by me* for *The Act of Roger Murgatroyd* and subsequently killed off *by me* in *A Mysterious Affair of Style*! I would surely have swooned had I not half-heard, from the eely black vortex into which I felt myself slide, Düttmann's voice whispering to me:

'Mr Adair, are you all right?'

'Yes, yes, I'm fine. The champagne . . . I'm virtually tee-total, you know. I oughtn't to have . . .'

'Not to worry. We are going into dinner now. You will feel better when you have eaten something hot.'

I walked into the dining room side by side with Düttmann, who was still anxiously gripping my elbow. Immediately ahead of us, arm in arm, were Slavorigin and Evie. He was telling her that he couldn't remember the name of the Sunday newspaper in which one of my whodunits had been very unfavourably reviewed and she, lowering her voice, said something which certainly sounded to me like 'P. D. James in the *Sunday Sundial*'. A few minutes later, as we stood round the table waiting to be advised by one of Düttmann's assistants where we were to be seated – there were no place settings – he proposed that they meet up again in London and asked for her telephone number, which he at once entered into his BlackBerry. This time I did clearly hear her answer. The number was Flaxman 3521.

He studied it on the BlackBerry's microscopic screen.

'I don't get it,' he said to Evie. 'Haven't you a flat in Albany?'

'As though!' she replied, mangling her colloquialisms as usual. 'That was just another of Gilbert's fabrications.'

'Ah yes, I remember. In *A Mysterious Affair of Style*. Didn't he describe it as "*the* Albany"? A strange solecism for someone so fond of calling himself a perfectionist.'

This I couldn't let pass, the more so as they appeared to be no longer troubled as to whether they were overheard or not.

'I knew quite well,' I said, 'that it should be referred to as "Albany", just "Albany". If I called it "the Albany" in the book, it's only because I didn't want to confuse the reader, who might have thought that Evie lived in the real Albany. I mean, the Albany in upstate New York.'

'As though!' sneered Slavorigin.

At dinner he completely dominated the conversation.

Oh, it was understandable that so world-famous an author should find himself fussed over as he was from the moment we entered the dining room. He was pointed out, not all that discreetly either, by more than one of our fellow diners and, even before we were all seated, an impetuous and enterprising adolescent girl in crotch-high shorts got up from her own crowded table, flounced over to ours and asked Slavorigin if he would consent to be photographed with her. He naturally did consent – I saw the minders stiffen at the tiny wallside table for two they were sharing – she handed a digital camera, along with basic instructions, to Sanary and flung her bare arms about a leering Slavorigin's neck. Later, when we started giving our orders to the *maître d'*, he requested, loud enough for the whole room to hear, a rare cheeseburger and a side-order of not French but freedom fries, a witticism that earned him a little round of applause.

It was during the meal itself, however, encouraged by an obsequious Düttmann, that he allowed nobody else to get a word in edgewise. To be honest, it was less his own fault than Düttmann's, who, unused to relaxing among a group of more or less equally distinguished off-duty writers, managed to transform what should have been a convivial get-together into an excuse to quiz the most distinguished of us all. It was like sitting in on a journalist's celebrity interview. Or on a dress rehearsal for the onstage discussion with Slavorigin that was scheduled to take place the following evening.

'Do you use a Mac or a PC?' 'A Mac.' 'What exactly does *Dark Jade* mean?' 'It's a title. Titles don't have to mean anything.' 'Which modern writer has most influenced you? Nabokov, perhaps?' '*Ah, celui-là, non!* Nabokov can't see the wood for the trees and too often he can't even see the trees for the mazy corrugation of their barks. It's as though he tried to corner the market in adjectival ethereality. Just riffle through *Lolita*. *Glossy, furry, honey-colored, honey-hued, honey-brown, leggy, slender, opalescent, russet, tingling, dreamy, biscuity, pearl-gray, hazy, flurry, dimpled, luminous, moist, silky, downy, shimmering, iridescent, gauzy, fragrant, coltish, nacreous, glistening, fuzzy, leafy, shady, rosy, dolorous, burnished, quivering, plumbacious, stippled*, and so on, and so forth. Do you know what that fabled style of his has always reminded me of? Fancy-schmancy restaurantese. Not a tomato that isn't sun-dried and honey-roasted! Not a scallop that isn't hand-dived and truffle-scented! The man must have shat marshmallows.' 'How incredibly funny and outrageous. But tell me please, in your internal exile have you ever given up hope? 'Ah, Tommy, *mein Lieber*, hope is as hard to give up as smoking.'

Düttmann finally enquired whether he was at work on a new novel. Slavorigin, now more than a little sozzled – he had also been taking a suspicious number of trips to the lavatory, accompanied by either Thomson or Thompson, it's true – answered that, yes, he was. 'Has it already got a title?' 'Not quite. I'm currently torn between *The Smell of the Lamp* – too Jamesian, perhaps? – and *The Vanishing Bookmark* – too Chestertonian? Or even *Moon Drop*. You get the allusion, I trust? In Latin *virus lunare*, a vaporous droplet shed by the moon on certain herbs under the influence of an incantation.' 'These,' said Düttmann, prudently sidestepping

144

the issue, 'are all first-rank titles.' 'Thank you. That must be why it's proving so hard to choose one over the other.' 'And may we ask what it's about?' 'Certainly. Would you [addressing all of us] really care to hear?' Nobody around the table dared to say no.

Now, it may have struck the reader that, throughout this memoir, I have been pretty rude about Gustav Slavorigin, even though, objectively speaking, and you needn't take only my word for it, he was a truly awful person. But I *am* willing to admit that, drunk and all, possibly even drugged to the eyeballs, when he actually did proceed to relate the plot of his new novel to us he held everybody at our table and several others in the seemingly bilingual dining room as spellbound as Wilde when reciting one of his apologues at the Café Royal.

'The book,' he began, 'consists of three separate sections:
'A Foreword;
'The Novel, plus Footnoted Annotations;
'An Afterword.
'In the Foreword the Author – let us call him G. – details the publishing history of the Novel itself. It was first brought out, he writes, by a small German-Swiss house based in Zurich, Epoca, as a work originally written in the German language and signed by the pseudonymous "D. J. Kadare" – no relation, needless to say, of the Albanian novelist and Nobelist-in-waiting Ismail. The following year, it was published in English by Faber & Faber as though it were a

translation from the German. It then started to appear in various other European countries, translated not from the English original but from the German translation. G., however, declines to explain why these subterfuges were necessary.

'He describes, instead, still rather enigmatically, his own personal need now to write an annotated version of this Novel, one which he realises is unlikely ever to be read by anybody but himself, at least in his own lifetime. It is, he insists, no mere authorial vanity which impels him to do so but a profound compulsion to commit to print the motive which had prompted him to launch upon such a book in the first place.

'The plot of the Novel – I mean the novel-within-my-novel – is of no importance. Or, if I may put that more candidly, I haven't yet decided what it's going to be, and it would only complicate matters anyway. I assure you, though, this is very much less of a barrier to your comprehension of the book as a whole than it may seem. All you need to know for the moment is that its title is *Apocalypso*.

'Of greater importance are the Footnotes. To start with, they mainly consist, as you would expect, of strictly informative annotations concerning the real names, places and events that are threaded through *Apocalypso* itself. Even at this early stage, however, the Reader notes a recurring tendency on G.'s part to confess that he took certain creative decisions – setting its opening section in a theatrical milieu, perhaps, and choosing a heterosexual protagonist – precisely because they belied his own public image as a homosexual theatre hater and baiter. It's also in the Footnotes that he reprints, like so many literary outtakes, a number of arresting metaphors that he admits to having reluctantly cut from the definitive draft. In fact, as the Reader gradually becomes aware, in a disorienting reversal of conventional practice, they are written in a denser and more overwrought style than the body of the text.

'Gradually, too, as they come to usurp more and more space on the page, the Reader discovers from the Footnotes that G., a much-lauded, best-selling, Booker-Prize-winning author, had earlier written an unpardonable book, a satirical denunciation of the culture and society of the contemporary United States whose closing chapter mercilessly debunked what he called "the burlesque cult of September 11".

'Even before the publication of that book, G. had had a handful of detractors like wolfhounds snapping at his heels. Now, because of it, there is actually a price on his head. A reclusive Texan billionaire, founder and funder of a nation-wide network of ultra-patriotic, ultra-hawkish organisations, has offered the reward of a hundred million dollars to anybody prepared to "terminate", to use his word, this arch-enemy of his beloved America. Since the threat could scarcely be more serious, G. at once goes to ground.

'He spends the next several months being shuttled from one safe house to another, from Watford to Hendon, from Leighton Buzzard to Welwyn Garden City. From these havens he issues frequent public statements in justification of his book. He plays endless games of Scrabble with his minders. He turns briefly to the Cross, but realises that it offers, for the unconditional freethinker he has always been, a hopelessly inadequate crutch. And it's when he has finally been driven close to suicidal despair by his nightmarish plight that a solution is proposed to him by an anonymous agent, known only as "Q", from MI6.

'"There exists,' says "Q" to G., 'but one means by which we can guarantee to prevent you from being murdered."

'"Which is?"

'"We murder you first."

'The logic, though maybe not immediately obvious, is nevertheless elementary. If the world were persuaded to believe – let us say, by an official statement of embarrassed regret from the British government – that G. has *already* been murdered, the Texas billionaire would undoubtedly call off his fatwa. G.'s facial features would then be remodelled by plastic surgery, he would be secretly transported out of England and assume a different identity in a different country.

'At first horrified by the prospect, G. eventually resigns himself to his fate.

'With his new face, and a new name to match, he moves into a well-appointed ranch-house, an *estancia*, the Villa Borgese, two hundred kilometres north of Buenos Aires. There, emancipated from the perpetual suspense of his peripatetic life in England, he lives contentedly enough for the first few months, reading, zapping the TV, pottering in the Villa's lushly overrun gardens. Except that there has, of course, been one imperative condition to his acceptance of this new existence of his. He has been forbidden to write, even more so to publish, a single word. His style is so instantly distinguishable from any other that, even under a pseudonym, he would sooner or later be tracked down.

'G. *is* a writer, however. He was born a writer, he will die a writer. Writing for him is not merely a profession, not merely a vocation, it's a natural, now almost physiological function, one he cannot for ever deny himself. And, one day, when he feels he can no longer tolerate such enforced autism, he conceives of a scheme, an absurdly grandiose scheme, whereby he may actually succeed in trumping fate. It's true, he owns to himself, that, even before the catastrophe had struck, his reputation was no longer what it had been. Reviewers and readers alike had wearied of magical realism, and their disaffection had been reflected in his once fabulous sales. So what, is his febrile thought, what if he were to exploit his predicament to do what he perhaps ought to have done a long time before – reinvent that too famous style of his?

'Where once his sentences had been luxuriantly long and serpentine, they would now become short and staccato. Where once his prose had been silvered by ripe, and some had said overripe, imagery, it would now be dry and lapidary.

Where once his pacing had been leisurely, it would now be rapid-fire. Of everything he had once done he would now do the opposite. Not only would such a contrarian strategy permit him to continue writing, even (why not?) publishing, not only would it maintain the secret of his true identity, it might even be his regeneration as an artist.

'And so it proved. Obliged, like the author of an anonymous letter, to camouflage his own all too distinctive *écriture*, he ruthlessly pruned his prose, focusing solely, even monomaniacally, on the stark self-sufficiency of the external world and thereby mining his way to a shining new simplicity.

'In the very last of the Footnotes, while informing the Reader how he also arranged, the better to cover his tracks, for *Apocalypso* to be published first in German translation and only afterwards in English, G. unexpectedly switches, quite literally in mid-sentence, to the present tense. He has just spotted a snow-white monoplane flying to and fro above the Villa Borgese. Later, on the same afternoon, having bicycled down into a nearby village to pick up supplies, he hears from local tradespeople that two American-accented strangers have been making enquiries about its tenant.

'And there both Novel and Footnotes end.

'There is, however, a brief Afterword. In this Afterword G. writes, still in the present tense, of the arrival at the *estancia* of the two Americans, of their cod-Pinteresque conversation with him and of his dawning realisation that their intention is indeed to kill him. Sinister yet at the same time unnervingly polite and accommodating, they allow him to complete the annotated edition of *Apocalypso* by writing, precisely, the Afterword the reader is in the process of reading. And G. himself takes the further opportunity of expressing his satisfaction that there is henceforth nothing to stop *Apocalypso* from being published at last under his own name.

'In the Afterword's closing paragraph G. recounts the very last minutes of his earthly existence. Considering all the precautions he took – changing his name, having his face surgically altered, living a loner's life in an obscure Argentinian province, publishing, and in German, a book which bore not the slightest resemblance to any work of fiction he had ever previously written – how, he asks his Nemeses, did they nevertheless contrive to track him down?

'"Why, sir," one of them smilingly replies, as though the response were self-evident, "it was your style. That style of yours is quite unmistakable."

'*Et voilà!*' concluded Slavorigin with all the corny panache of a professional conjuror.

His bravura performance, which I have to say it was, prompted still more applause from virtually the entire dining room, in which, as I had failed to realise, so raptly attentive had I myself been to his storytelling, hardly a word had been exchanged for twenty minutes or so. At our own table, on the other hand, the reaction was, shall we say, mixed. From neither Meredith nor Autry, for example, could be detected any sign of enthusiasm at all.

After responding to Düttmann's 'Bravo!' with a charming little bow, Slavorigin addressed the former.

'So, Merry,' he asked her in a voice that had turned slurry again, something it hadn't been during his filibuster, 'what did you think?'

'You know what I think!' she snapped back at him.

'No, I don't. How could I?'

'You know how repulsive I found *Out of a Clear Blue Sky*. Okay, a lot of bad stuff has happened since then and maybe we've all come to feel differently about things, I know I have, but even so, even so, for you to be so fucking callous and conceited as to return to your offence, an offence some of us might just have been willing to forgive, to return to it like a dog to its doo-doos, no, no, that I can't take!'

The whole room fell deathly quiet. I felt Evie's eyes on all of us and on me above all.

'And what offence is that?'

'The "poetry of September 11"! For Christ's sake, those were real people who died in the Towers! Those were real people who leapt to their certain deaths one after the other! "Like globs of wax dripping from two tall twin candles"! That's what you wrote, isn't it? Globs of wax? It's disgusting.'

'Do try not to misquote me. What I wrote was "globules of wax".'

'How dare you make poetry, so-called poetry, out of human agony! How dare you say "They're only Americans, after all"!'

'No hypocrisy, please, Meredith,' he said. 'When you open your *LA Times* and you see a headline, assuming the *LA Times* even bothers to publish such a headline, about some genocidal massacre in Serbia or Sudan, let's be honest now, don't you yawn and think, "Oh well, they're only Serbians or Sudanese" and at once turn the page?'

'Of course I don't!'

'Quite right, you don't. You don't even have to. You don't have to think anything at all. For you Americans indifference to the suffering of others has become so instinctive it's not even a tic.'

'You really are a scumbag.'

'I may be a scumbag,' answered Slavorigin, a hard and dangerous glitter in his eyes. 'I'm also an artist, an aesthete. You talk of making poetry out of human agony. Tell me, how long do you suppose Tennyson waited before writing "The Charge of the Light Brigade"?'

Since Meredith made no reply, he swept the table with a glance.

'No? Nobody? Spaulding? How long?'

'Haven't the foggiest,' Hugh said with a soft belch.

'Guess.'

'I dunno. Obviously not long, etc, etc, or you wouldn't be asking the question. A year? Six months?'

'*Minutes!*' Slavorigin all but shrieked at us. 'According to his grandson, Tennyson wrote "The Charge of the Light Brigade" a matter of minutes after reading a reporter's account of the massacre in *The Times*. He waited minutes, I waited five years. A day will dawn,' he continued tipsily, 'a day will dawn when the poetry of September 11 has become a cliché. I'm just ahead of my time as usual. '

'Who gives a shit about Tennyson? Remember what Adorno said –' Meredith rejoined the conversation before being immediately interrupted.

'Why must one *always* quote Adorno to me? "To write poetry after Auschwitz is barbaric", right? But there has been plenty of poetry after Auschwitz, poetry and prose and drama and ballet and film and music. What moronic presumption, attempting to dictate to the future how it can or cannot behave. Are we to mourn in perpetuity? Till the end of time? It's intolerable! The Holocaust has become a religion, an old-time, Old Testament religion of hellfire and damnation, a religion whose Original Sin is the Final Solution. Well, I for one refuse any longer to atone for an offence I never committed.'

With a trembling hand he drew a cigarette from Hugh's half-open pack of Marlboros and lit it from the small bronze edelweiss-shaped candle that was our table's centrepiece.

'Anyway, I wasn't even the first.'

'The first what?' I asked.

'The first to extract poetry from September 11. Although, to be fair, the poem in question was written some forty years before the event itself occurred and a minor adjustment – oh, no more than three or four words – must be made first.'

'What is this poem you're referring to?'

'Come, Gilbert, have you forgotten the opening quatrain of Nabokov's *Pale Fire*?

'*I was the shadow of the waxwing slain*
'*By the false azure in the window pane –*'

'As I say, all it needs is a minor adjustment.

'*I was the shadow of the hijacked plane*
'*By the false azure in the window slain –*'

'Stop him, somebody!' Meredith cried out.

'*I was the smudge of ashen fluff – and I*
'*Lived on, flew on, in the reflected sky.*'

An ugly, sarcastic grin disfigured the lower half of his still beautiful face.

'"The smudge of ashen fluff". How vividly prescient of sly old VN, don't you agree?'

Hurling her napkin onto the table, exactly as I remembered her doing at that little straw-roofed, sun-dappled beach restaurant in Antibes, Meredith stood up and, without a word of apology to Düttmann, or to the rest of us for that matter, stalked out of the dining room. I caught Evie's eye. There was a momentary drop in tension as if our table had struck an air pocket.

Although he had undoubtedly won the argument, quite literally seen Meredith off, Slavorigin didn't at that moment have the air or aura of a victor. He had a killjoy's mean and petulant expression on his face and I suspect, given his natural and of course now long-frustrated gregarity, and despite his well-documented relish for controversy, he had not on this occasion actively sought to provoke a squabble, thereby spoiling the evening for everyone, and had hoped instead that the résumé of his new novel would have prompted such warmth and sincerity of praise it would remain uncontaminated by the lingering rancour of old enmities. His vanity as a writer, a creative artist, an aesthete, as he had just defined himself, had been badly wounded and for once, in public, he cut an almost pitiful figure.

It was to me he spoke next.

'Gilbert, what did you think of it?'

'I liked it a lot. I particularly admired the way you write, or plan to write, on a theme which is very close to you, even autobiographical, yet you manage to distance yourself from that theme through the novel's form and also, I presume, its language.'

'Autobiographical, eh? Perhaps. Except that I haven't been murdered.'

For a brief instant the word 'yet' seemed to hover between us.

'Mrs Trubshawe?' he said to Evie.

'Oh, delightful, quite delightful!' she trilled. 'If a bit over my head, you know.'

'Sanary?' (Hugh's opinion, probably to Hugh's own relief, seemed not to interest him.) 'Is this yet another of my "borrowings" in your view?'

'No comment,' Sanary silkily answered him. 'But please,' he added, 'don't take that personally. It's my nature. Rather, it's my nationality. Like all of my compatriots, I was born neutral. If I offered you an opinion, I would instantly cease to be Swiss.'

'In other words, blah blah blah.'

He finally turned to Autry.

'What about you, laughing boy? Have you nothing to say?'

'Well, okay, I'll tell you,' Autry eventually replied, removing the toothpick from his mouth. 'I read your book. *Out of a Clear Blue Sky*? Yeah, I read it all right. We all did. And, you know what, I felt a lot of hatred in that book, a *lot* of hatred. What they call self-hatred.'

'*Self*-hatred?!' echoed a stupefied Slavorigin.

'That's what I said. For me it was a book by somebody who really *loves* America, but hates himself for loving it.'

Although I myself thought this to be pure dollar-book Freud, I overheard Sanary whisper to Evie, '*Nom d'un nom!* I think he is – how you say? – right.'

After dinner we were all, Meredith excepted, chauffeured back into town and, as had been promised by Düttmann, on to its one and only disco. A disco, I call it, but it was no ordinary disco. By coincidence, considering the setting of

Slavorigin's new novel, what was danced there, by men and women, by men and men, also by women and women, was the horniest dance in the world, the Argentinian tango.

We commandeered a ringside table, ordered what everybody else seemed to have ordered, Bacardi-and-Cokes all round, and settled down to enjoy as we could the smoky spectacle.

But even before we were served our drinks, an almost hiplessly slim young stranger, not effeminate though obviously gay, wearing a white vest that clung wetly to his breastplate of a chest and a pair of chinos so loose about the waist we could read the brand name of his white underpants, approached our table and asked Slavorigin if he cared to dance. Thomson and Thompson were having a quiet drink at the bar, but their charge turned to the rest of us as if we had some sort of right to mind. We, or some of us, managed to eke out glassy smiles of benediction and, hands clasped, they strode onto the floor.

God, they were good! Slavorigin really did know how to dance. I watched him as he and his partner clamped themselves onto each other's now electrically taut, now sensual and yielding torso. I watched how, his head tossed back, he would brusquely stamp his feet in a ferocious tango tantrum while his partner raised a single black boot behind him, casting a furtive glance at its heel as though in fear that he might have trod on something unmentionable. I watched too how, glissando after glissando, every joint and pivot of their bodies would click magnetically together, before terminating in a perfectly timed four-legged splits.

When, still hand in hand, they walked back off the floor, Slavorigin whispered in the ear of the sweaty young stranger, who began smiling and nodding, just smiling and nodding. Then, as they were about to reach our table, they abruptly unclasped hands and went their separate ways. Watching his partner disappear into the crowd, Slavorigin reclaimed his seat beside us, his long legs sprawling sexily under the table.

I myself slipped unobtrusively away half an hour later, and I have no idea when the evening ended for the others.

Chapter Eight

Dreams like hallucinations divine and speak to our fear of dying, and sleep, as many have written before me, is the green room of the hereafter.* That night I slept fitfully. On one of my room's twin bedside tables I had earlier in the evening laid out a brand new sleeping-mask and a pair of *boules Quiès*, by then as grey and tough as wads of chewed-out gum. Now, wandering naked into the bathroom to brush my teeth, swallow a blood-pressure pill and take one last pee for the road, I switched on the alarm-clock radio and located a sort of classical-music channel: Honegger's *Pacific 231* followed by the 'big tune' of a Rachmaninov piano concerto, etc. Although I had packed a snug little compact-disc player along with three favourite late-night

---

* Interestingly, it has long been rumoured of Hermann Hunt V that, being of too craven a disposition to ingest any of the better-known mind-altering substances but curious none the less to experience their effect, he once paid – handsomely, as usual – a locally based avant-gardist theatrical troupe to 'act out' a series of hallucinations in front of him. I personally have never believed the story.

discs, whenever I am about to sleep alone, away from home, I do prefer the radio to records. *Somebody is out there.*

It was close to midnight when I slid beneath the duvet. As predicted, I had to wrestle with the bolster, wedging it under the nape of my neck (which made me feel as though I were in a barber's chair), piling a second bolster on top of the first (a dentist's chair), then experimenting at length to discover whether it might be practical to dispense with the damn things altogether (a coffin). At last, *faute de mieux*, I arrived at a tolerable position by clasping one of them to my jawline like a violinist his violin.

Only after these and other such threshings, turning my face over on my left cheek then my right cheek then my left again, then, as a despairing last resort, trying to sleep flat on my back, my eyes sightlessly open under the already sticky mask, then getting up twice to fiddle with the radiator's complicated thermostat – the room abruptly revealed itself to be suffocatingly warm, something I seemed not to have noticed before – only then did I succeed in losing consciousness. And I was no sooner asleep, so it felt, than I started to dream.

Now for me all dreams, *all dreams*, are nightmares; there is, I find, a denaturingly strange and suggestive something about the state-of-the-art scene-shifting of even the prosiest of dreamscapes, just as in the staidest of surrealist paintings. Hence, however unscary this dream of mine may strike the reader, it was from my point of view a nightmare none the less. I didn't wake up screaming but, when I finally did surface, I feared at first I would have to vomit.

I dreamt I was in Switzerland (a less logical and realistic setting than it may appear, since the semi-self-aware 'I' who was doing the dreaming was *not* in Switzerland but in Notting Hill, dreams like mobile phones tending to adopt the default assumption that the dreamer is in his own territory). This dream-Switzerland was a picture-postcard platitude, from which not one of Hitchcock's clichés was missing, not even the village-square dance, the whirl of dirndl, on which curtains used to rise in nineteenth-century operettas. It also had a Swiss-themed soundtrack, Rossini's *William Tell* Overture.

Naked, then again sometimes fully clothed, I was being chased across a Tobleronish range of small, no more than knee-high, perfectly triangular mountains, the foothills of the infinite, by somebody or something whose contours I couldn't at first make out with exactitude. The chase, moreover, was a very uneven one. For a while he, if he it were (but I gradually came to understand that my pursuer was indeed male), appeared to glide above the mountains in a sustained and seamless arc underneath a sky of tampons and rainbows, while I found myself obliged by my dream's martinet of a *metteur-en-scène* to plod over the lovely, dark, deep snow (shades of Frost!) at the much more pedestrian pace of a cross-country skier. There couldn't be any doubt, then, that he would catch up with me.

And he kept coming. Without even having to turn my head, I somehow knew that he was dressed in the garb – quilted anorak, its fur-lined hood reposing on his slightly stooped shoulders, old-fashioned khaki shorts and thick woollen stockings which nearly met those shorts halfway up his chubby legs – of a portly butterfly-hunter. In actual fact (if I can use that phrase about a dream), he wasn't chasing me after all. Waving his long-stemmed net every which way, he was endeavouring to nab a colony of butterflies that waltzed insouciantly around his head as though dangled on as many strings. And it was only when he was about to overtake me that I realised that the butterflies weren't butterflies at all but books, open books, their pages fluttering in the wind-machine breeze. I could even read their titles, about most of which, however, there seemed to me something not quite right. *Pnun* was one. Another was *Son of Palefire*. A third, which I caught sight of at the very instant he snared the book, was *Adair or Ardor*.

At that same instant, as Rossini's overture swelled on the soundtrack and the shadow of my pursuer's net cast its own net over me, he morphed into the Lone Ranger. Wearing a black sleeping-mask just like mine, brandishing in his right hand the butterfly-net with the captured and still vainly fluttering book inside it, the book which bore my name, digging a bejewelled spur into his horse's tender haunch so that it reared up on its two hind legs, he cried out, 'Hi-Yo, Silver!' Then, accompanied by his faithful pard Tonto (now where had he sprung from?), he galloped away on thundering hoofbeats into the thrilling days of yesteryear and I awoke.

When I consulted my wristwatch, I was shocked to discover that it was twenty-five past eleven and that, over-sleeping as I had, I risked missing altogether the Mayor's reception which would already be well underway. I leapt out of bed, raced into the bathroom and, twelve minutes later, a personal record, had shaved, showered and dressed. Breakfast was no longer being served in the dining room, nor would I have had time to consume it even if it were, and my hope was that coffee as well as alcohol would be available at the Kunsthalle.

I rushed downstairs, through the lobby and out into the car park. Ignoring the appeals of my palpitating heart to take it easy, I ran straight to the Kunsthalle building, which I made out ahead of me every step of the way but which still felt unpleasantly distant for one as out-of-shape as I was.

As I drew closer, I saw a crowd of people with glasses of champagne in their hands, some I knew, others not, milling about on its front steps. I recognised Sanary, his blazer a black blot among so many pastel shades, and the ubiquitous Evie, and I heard a loud drawl – 'I tell you, he's ghaarstly, he's perfectly ghaarstly!' – which told me that Meredith too was of the company. A minute later I myself was among them.

'What's happened?' I breathily asked.

As I might have foreseen, Evie was the first to reply.

164

'It's Slavorigin.'

'What about him?'

'He's disappeared.'

'Disappeared? What do you mean, disappeared?'

What I learned from her was that Slavorigin had so far failed to put in an appearance at the reception which had been organised in his honour. For a while everybody had sought to stay calm and convivial. By twenty-past eleven, however, it had become impossible to continue pretending that his ongoing absence was no cause for alarm, and some-body – 'I fancy,' she said, 'it was Pierre here' – suggested that Düttmann return at once to the Hilton to find out whether and when Slavorigin had left it. But just as he was preparing to go, who should turn up at the Kunsthalle but Thomson and Thompson, 'neither of them a happy bunny'. At a quar-ter to eleven they had knocked on Slavorigin's door to escort him to the reception, even though the Kunsthalle was just a five-minute stroll away. No response. They had then taken the lift back down to the ground floor to ask the reception-ist whether Mr Slavorigin by chance had already gone. They were told no, that he would certainly have been seen cross-ing the lobby area. One of them – let's say it was Thompson – took the lift back up to the twelfth floor while his twin remained behind at the reception desk. A couple of minutes later Thomson's mobile phone rang. It was Thompson to say that there was still no response. Accompanied by Thomson, the manager himself then took the lift up and unlocked the bedroom door with his own set of keys. All three entered the room together. No Slavorigin. On which, alert to the implications of what they stubbornly refused to admit could have been their own professional negligence, the two low-rent minders set off for the Kunsthalle in the hope that their charge had somehow contrived to exit the hotel unnoticed.

And that's where things stood when I arrived. Düttmann, I saw, was talking in whispers to an extremely tall, straight-backed man in a double-breasted suit, a sort of General De Gaulle with some of the excess air let out, whom I took (correctly) to be the Mayor. G. Autry, in an outfit not unlike that worn by the Lone Ranger in my dream, minus mask and revolver, was being spoken at by one of Düttmann's assistants, a gawky, bespectacled, pony-tailed brunette whose fidgety smile testified, even from as far away from them as I myself stood, to her fear of being reprimanded for having left one of the Festival's guests, if only for a few minutes, to his own devices. Meredith, who kept darting glances at me, was feigning interest in what a gesticulating Hugh had to say to her. (Though I found it hard to credit, particularly under the circumstances, it did cross my mind that this might be a new attempt of his to borrow the ten thousand pounds he was so direly in need of.) And the two bodyguards were looking woebegone indeed.

What was to be done? After a deal of verbal to-ing and fro-ing, it was Sanary who came up with a sensible suggestion.

'We should,' he said, 'take a look in the Museum.'

'Why do you say the Museum, Monsieur Sanary?' Dütt-mann asked, his gammy eye blinking violently.

'In this town there is nowhere else, it seems to me, that he could have gone. It's the Museum or the Falls. And since the Museum is the nearer of the two, that's where we should proceed first.'

Although nothing audible was said for or against his proposal, the general babble that followed sounded more approving than not and we all began to shuffle across to the Museum, which, like virtually everything else in Meiringen, was located just six or seven hundred yards away.

A queer thing occurred *en route*. I was walking between Evie and Meredith, and I spotted, on the far side of the narrow street, the twin toddlers from the flight whom I had already seen twenty-four hours earlier, seated with their parents on the café terrace. What startled me on this occasion, what really rather disturbed me, was that they were unchaperoned. A pair of foreign two-year-olds alone in the main street of a Swiss resort? What could their parents be thinking of? And where in God's name were they? As warmly wrapped up as before, matching little bobble hats on matching little heads, the twins waddled happily along the pavement in the direction opposite that in which our party was headed, towing in their parallel wakes two identical wooden Donald Ducks with wheels instead of feet and heads which would metronomically nod, up and down, up and down, as they advanced. Perhaps they also quacked; I was too far away to hear. As I tried to point out to my not at all interested companions, it was most extraordinary.

Our stroll to the Museum took six minutes. Just as had been the case when I visited it with Düttmann and Spaulding, the box-office was unmanned, a dereliction of duty which elicited tut-tuts from the Mayor and his entourage. We started to file in one by one, there being a turnstile to manoeuvre, one we might have expected to prohibit entry to us visitors without tickets, but in fact it didn't. I was fifth in the queue. Düttmann, two of his female assistants and somebody else I couldn't place were in front of me; Hugh, a plume of his chain-smoker's breath coiling about my earlobes, behind me; Evie and Meredith, if I remember aright, behind him.

Suddenly we all heard Düttmann cry out. One of his assistants began screaming and the queue heaved up with a judder. I had already squeezed through the turnstile and now hastened into the main gallery, that room-size replica of the Baker Street rooms that Holmes shared with Watson. At first I could see nothing but the unnaturally stiffened postures of those who had preceded me and who were standing stock-still in a little semi-circle. Düttmann's two young assistants were holding their hands cupped over their mouths, the profiles of their frighteningly white faces made visible to me by their both having turned away in horror from whatever spectacle it was that confronted them. Düttmann himself was trembling; and as I rather blunderingly, I fear, pushed past him to see what they had all stumbled upon, he sought momentary support from the high-backed chair that served Watson's mahogany writing desk.

Deaf to the confused hubbub behind me, as the others continued to step gingerly into the cramped room, I looked down at the figure on the carpet. It was of course Slavorigin. As soon as I saw him, I knew why people said 'as dead as a doornail'. It was almost as though his body had actually been nailed to the ground. The beautiful face lying sideways, half on the carpet, half on the exposed surround of the wooden floor, was expressionless: no terror, not even a hint of surprise, could be detected in features more serene than I ever remembered them to have been in his mostly angry life. Clearly, he never knew he had died and was still none the wiser.

Gustav Slavorigin dead! What an almighty stink this would cause! But the worst was to come. The din inside the room was now indescribable, as everybody in turn got an eyeful of the corpse, reacting with a shriek or a muffled moan or a stammered 'Oh my God!'. Evie, who had been here before, as it were, albeit only between the covers of my whodunits, looked much more squeamish than I had described her in print, even in *A Mysterious Affair of Style*, whose murder victim was, after all, supposed to be her oldest and dearest friend, and I heard Autry muttering a guttural 'Jesus!' again and again under his breath. Then quite by chance, as if the reels of Time were being changed, there came upon us all one of those unheralded instants of synchronised hush, the whole room falling silent at once, and Sanary pointed downward at the body and said in a bold clear voice, 'Look!'

A queerly spindly object was sticking out of Slavorigin's chest, an object that had come close to splitting in the middle as he fell. I suppose that, if I hadn't immediately been conscious of it, it was because I'd naturally been drawn first, as one is, to the face. Or perhaps even then I'd had a premonition of some abnormality, an obscenely protruding bone, for example, that I would live to regret too intently focusing upon. Not that I really did think it was a bone; I didn't 'think' anything. But an internal whisper, bypassing the speculative turmoil of my brain, may have insinuated to me that this – this *thing* had to be a bone, for what else could it be?

It was an arrow. We could all now clearly see the tuft of faded, mangy turkey feathers which had been glued or fletched, I believe the technical term is, to the blunt end of its shaft. It was, in fact, as a backward glance instantly confirmed, the very arrow, with its crudely daubed-on bloodstain, that I had inspected the previous day on the half-moon table where it had lain next to the hundred-year-old copy of the *Daily Telegraph* and the pulpy edition of *His Last Bow*, both of them, incidentally, undisturbed.

There was a collective gasp, as from the audience at the kind of movie where a blonde co-ed opens a closet door and the dead Dean topples into her scantily pantied lap like a felled oak. Sanary knelt down and, without even bothering to brace himself for the shock, gently turned Slavorigin's body over. Another, louder gasp. The arrow was stuck deep in his chest, so deep it seemed to have acted as a stopper: the blood that soaked his blue-and-white striped shirt was far less than one would have expected. Tiny bubbles speckled with foamy pink saliva drooled from his gaping mouth. Yet his expression, as I said before, was as unalarmed as if he'd been shot in the back.

'You know,' said Evie in a quiet voice, 'you really shouldn't have done that.'

Sanary looked up at her, pale-faced.

'Done what?'

'You don't have to be a reader of whodunits to know that you must never take the liberty of touching a dead body before the police arrive.'

He hastily yanked both his hands from off Slavorigin's snakeskin jacket as if only just realising that it was now being worn by a corpse. But by then it was too late.

During the whole of that afternoon, right there in the Kunst-halle's lecture hall, we were all questioned by a local police inspector, Schumacher by name. Fiftyish, weedily built, with a tiny, Hitlerian clump of a moustache, he was quite without the stoic morbidity of Swiss policemen in Dürrenmatt's thrillers. On the contrary. He actually seemed to regard it as a source of perverse pride that such a celebrated author should have been shot dead (with William Tell's bow-and-arrow, for God's sake!) in his own boring backwater of a town.

What was most curious about the interviews – 'interrogations' is hardly the word – was that not one of us turned out to have an altogether satisfactory alibi. Not that we all fell under suspicion, as the tacit consensus was that Slavorigin had obviously been slain by a fanatic. The main autobahn out of Meiringen was already under surveillance and all Swiss airports were being patrolled by anti-terrorist units, every wing in the sky accounted for. According to the police doctor's preliminary report, however, the victim had died within an hour, at most an hour-and-a-half, of our having discovered him, and by some impish coincidence, as I say, not one of us could offer a truly secure alibi for that little skylight window of opportunity.

Meredith, who was up first, told Schumacher that before finally gravitating to the Kunsthalle she had spent the morning wandering about the town's rather disappointing shopping precinct. Yes, she had been alone and, no, she hadn't made any purchases, but she had spoken to the odd shop assistant who might be able to vouch for her. Sanary had taken breakfast in the hotel, also on his own, then returned to his bedroom to pick up his emails. He had not responded to any of them, with the result that nothing of his could be traced or timed, assuming anybody thought it worth doing so. His next hour was spent jotting down preliminary notes on the first three chapters of a children's fantasy novel he had been commissioned to translate from the English, *The Master of the Fallen Chairs*, and although he had hung a *Bitte nicht stören* sign on his bedroom door he had forgotten, or so he thought, to remove it when he eventually did leave, at five to eleven. No, no, hold on there, he suddenly said. About quarter of an hour earlier a chambermaid had tapped on his door only for him to request that she come back later. Autry, whom I had never heard string so many articulate sentences together at one go, admitted to having mooched about the Reichenbach Falls for an hour or two, alone naturally, although he had noticed, but had also deliberately steered clear of, the usual mob of sightseers. Hugh claimed to have awakened late, if not as late as I had, and been disturbed by the same chambermaid. There was also in his account, for me at least, one piquant detail which would have definitively convinced me of his innocence had I ever imagined anybody might have considered him guilty. If he overslept, he said, it was only because, owing to his unfamiliarity with continental bolsters and duvets, he had taken forever to drift off the night before. I, too, had of course slept late. And Evie, the very last of us to be interviewed – Düttmann and his trio of assistants were out of the running, having all naturally observed each other making last-minute preparations for the

Kunsthalle reception – told Schumacher that she had traipsed for almost an hour from one news kiosk to another in an attempt to find a copy of an English newspaper.

'Any particular newspaper?' he asked.

'The *Daily Sentinel*,' she to my astonishment replied.

'And did you find it?'

'Why yes, I finally did. At the railway station. Should have tried there first.'

'It would be of assistance to me, *gnädige Frau*, if you still had that copy in your possession.'

'Ah well,' said Evie, 'I'm afraid I haven't. You see, I took it with me to the station cafeteria and read it over a cappuccino. Then – what? – yes, I dumped it in a litter bin and walked to the Kunsthalle. On the way, though, I did pop into a souvenir shop to ask the price of a glass paperweight – it contained a miniature Mont Blanc, you know, which I thought I might buy for my godson's birthday – but that was just before I arrived here, at exactly eleven o'clock. Sorry.'

The *Daily Sentinel*? What new nonsense was this? Couldn't she any longer distinguish the fictional Evadne Mount from the real live Evie? Or was she so flustered by Schumacher's affable drilling of her she absent-mindedly named one of the spurious, jokily named newspapers I had invented for my whodunits? Pish posh! She hadn't been flustered at all. She had been as cool as the proverbial cucumber – gaarh, now I'm doing it! I was determined to have the matter out with her later, privately.

There was one last, token question which we all had put to us before we were permitted to go about our respective affairs, but only those affairs, mark you, that could be conducted within the strict confines of Meiringen itself. Not, as Schumacher once more took pains to reassure us, that any of us was considered a suspect, but he expected from one hour to the next the arrival from Brussels of a senior official from Interpol – Interpol versus the Internet? I know which I would bet my money on – as also two British intelligence agents, and, begging our pardons, he could not be expected to dismiss us until the three of them had seen for themselves what was and what wasn't what. I was rather amused to hear that a Belgian detective would soon be on the murderer's trail. It struck me that, with Evie already *in situ*, his presence would belatedly represent the fulfilment of that ancient dream of all Christie fans, a whodunit in which Marple and Poirot, as rival sleuths, endeavour simultaneously to solve the same crime.*

And the token question? Slavorigin had definitely been shot, not stabbed, and we all knew where the arrow had come from, but the bow? A bow is not an easy thing to conceal. It's a big object, usually, bigger than you would expect, and whether it's fashioned of wood or plastic it mustn't be bent too far lest it split or, scarcely less serious, cause the

---

* Which of the two would come out on top? I was reminded of the old metaphysical conundrum: Can God, who after all can do everything, create an object so heavy not even He can lift it off the ground?

arrow to be so erratically propelled as to be, even at a short distance, deflected from its target. These facts were communicated to us by Schumacher himself, something of an expert, it seemed. He went on:

'Now the Reichenbach Falls, which you all know, they are the obvious – no, they are the *only* safe place to cast away the bow after it has been employed. But Monsieur Autre has just told us that he spent this morning mooshing about' – a touch of Clouseau here – 'at the Falls and so it is difficult for me to comprehend how our killer can then discard his arm, his weapon, in security. You understand me, yes?' (We all nodded.) 'So I must ask you this last question. Have any of you espied such a bow in Meiringen?' (Lots of head-shakes.) 'Then, ladies and gentlemen, you are free to go on your ways. But, I repeat, for now you must remain here inside our town. If not for a long time, I hope.'

Outside, on the steps of the Kunsthalle, I asked Hugh, for want of something better to do that afternoon, if he played chess. He didn't. He counter-proposed a game of poker, suggesting that we make up a foursome with Autry and Sanary, but, like Bartleby, I preferred not to. I still meant anyway to have my say with Evie, whom I was determined not to let out of my sight. She was conversing with Meredith, and I heard the latter address her as 'Y'all' and she wasn't even from the South! What an astounding woman Evie was.

It was near the bronze Sherlock Holmes, as she was

trudging back to the hotel on her own, that I eventually caught up with her.

'Evie,' I said, panting slightly, 'there you are.'

'Ah, Gilbert. So tell me, what do you make of all this?'

'Frankly, I still can't believe it's happened. What about you?'

'Likewise. In fact, I was just returning to my room to think it through. Perhaps we could meet up later in the bar. At cocktail hour.'

'Of course, of course. It's just . . .'

'What?'

'Just that I wanted to ask you a question.'

'Fire away.'

'In the Kunsthalle,' I said, trying to sound offhand, 'when you were interviewed by Schumacher . . .'

'Yes?'

'You told him you'd spent most of the morning looking for a newspaper.'

'That's right. I did.'

'Um, what was its name again?'

'Its name?'

'The newspaper's name.'

'The *Daily Sentinel*. Why?'

'The *Daily Sentinel*. I see. And you finally did find it at the railway station?'

'Yes, I did. What is this all about, Gilbert?'

'Evie,' I said as composedly as I could, 'I've never heard of a newspaper called the *Daily Sentinel*. A real newspaper, that is.'

She contemplated me for a moment or two.

'What daily newspaper do *you* read?'

'Why,' I replied, caught off-guard, 'the *Guardian*.'

'Well, there you are. I never heard of that either.'

'You've never heard of the *Guardian*?!'

'The *Guardian*? Guardian of what, I wonder.'

'It's a world-famous newspaper!'

'If you say so, Gilbert, if you say so,' she answered with an exasperating smirk.

'Tell me,' I ventured, now less and less willing to humour her, 'I suppose you also take a regular Sunday paper?'

'Naturally.'

'Which one?'

'The *Sunday Sundial*,' was her answer, as of course I knew it would be. Then, adopting a brusque businesslike tone, she said, 'Gilbert, I'd love to continue this fascinating chat with you, but I really do have a lot of mulling over to do. Shall we say six o'clock in the hotel bar?'

Without another word she left me standing alone in the deserted street.

I myself didn't return at once to the Hilton. Instead, I wandered over to the railway station where I soon found its modestly cosmopolitan news kiosk. After purchasing a packet of Dunhills, I asked the young man who served me, his eyes a mystery under the shade of a scarlet baseball cap, if he happened to stock a copy of the *Daily Sentinel*. He didn't, but I'd be lying if I pretended he didn't first riffle through various publications I had already noticed on the foreign-newspaper stand – *The Times, Telegraph, Independent, Guardian* – before shaking his head.

'Sold out,' he said in English.

At an adjacent ice-cream parlour I bought myself a giant bicephalic cone – pistachio and apricot – and slowly made my way back to the hotel.

Chapter Nine

'Heavens to Murgatroyd!'

It was a lovely fresh sky-blue morning, and Evie and I were seated on two grubby plastic white chairs on the terrace of the same café in which I had had a coffee and chat with Düttmann, Sanary and Hugh Spaulding the day of my arrival. Only thirty-eight hours ago! It was not to be believed. The once drowsy little Meiringen was crawling with plainclothes police agents, Swiss but also no doubt British, whom we tried to single out from holidaying promenaders. From time to time, the fanfare of a siren would wail way off on the far side of town, an odd occurrence in a place where formerly the loudest noise would have been the routine peal of church bells. Every so often, too, our voices, even Evie's, were outroared by the drilling of construction workers who had started digging up both transverse thoroughfares of the junction on which the café was situated. Not for the first time I fantasised about patenting a device to fit silencers to pneumatic drills as to firearms.

The previous evening, as agreed, she and I had met in the hotel bar for cocktails. I was unable, however, to pump her on the matter, which had nagged at me since we parted, of her favourite newspaper. I had been looking forward to firing one question after another at her – what was the *Daily Sentinel*'s politics? How much did it cost? Broadsheet or tabloid? Names and opinions of star columnists? – in the hope of causing her to trip up somewhere along the way. But no sooner had we ordered drinks than we were joined by Sanary and Hugh, who had taken the lift down together, and the conversation had immediately turned to Slavorigin's death and how long we might expect to be held under what was coming to seem tantamount to house, or hotel, arrest.

Hugh's accent, I couldn't help remarking, mysteriously came and went, like that of an insecure English actor miscast in Synge or O'Casey, depending on whether he was speaking to Evie (all hammy Oirishry) or to me (nary a trace of Irishness, which was surely to be expected after so many years lived in England); while Sanary, hearing that Evie had not after all spent the afternoon cogitating in her room, as she assured me she would, but propping up the bar, drawing out not merely the two disgraced minders but the Museum ticket-issuer, a whiny white-haired pensioner who insisted to her that he had absented himself for no more than ten minutes because of a spongy bladder, cried '*Zut alors!* I doff my hat, Madame!' Whereupon he doffed an imaginary topper, and I thought I would go mad.

Then a despondent Düttmann entered the bar and our party eventually drifted into the hotel's own restaurant, in which we consumed a none too animated supper before, with perceptible relief on all sides, retiring early.

Coming back to the present, as I had said not a word in response to her exclamation, Evie repeated it, although this time it was more in the nature of a sigh.

'Heavens to Murgatroyd!'

'A penny for your thoughts.'

'I was thinking,' she replied, 'what a rum affair this has turned out to be. For me above all.'

'Oh. And why you above all?'

'Well, think about it yourself. It seems increasingly to be the case that – just like Alexis Baddeley, the regular detective in my own whodunits, you remember – wherever I happen to be, I find myself infallibly stumbling across a murder. It's almost as though it were some kind of a Law, and I'm starting to wonder whether we aren't – I mean me, Alexis, Father Brown, Hercule Poirot, Jane Marple – I'm starting to wonder whether the trait shared by us amateur or professional sleuths, the secret trait nobody ever dares mention, is that we're all *jinxes*.'

'Jinxes?'

'Think about it, I say. We all solve murders, true, but it should be obvious to fans of mystery fiction that we also *create the conditions* for these murders simply by being there, whether in a snowed-in country house on Dartmoor or on an archaeological dig in Mesopotamia or indeed in an idyllic little town in the Swiss Alps. In fact, you might even say that we have a moral obligation to solve them because they'd doubtless not have been committed in the first place had we not been on the scene.

'You know, that insight of mine has just given me another idea, an idea so ingenious I might actually use it as the theme of my next whodunit, ha! ha! My regular police inspector, my Trubshawe, if you will – his name, as you may or may not recall, is Tomlinson, Tomlinson of the Yard – well now, let me see, I might have him sitting in his club one evening, nursing all the bruises his self-esteem has received over the years at his having been so consistently outsleuthed by Alexis. Suddenly it dawns on him that the one thread, the only meaningful thread, connecting all the murders she has solved in her lengthy career is her own fortuitous, or *allegedly* fortuitous, presence at the scene of each and every one of the crimes. So, in the very last chapter, he naturally arrests her as the most subtle and successful serial killer in history.'

'Are you serious?' I asked, genuinely impressed. (With Evie, you never knew.)

Shaking her head, she took a sip of her cappuccino.

'No. Only kidding. My readers wouldn't stand for it.'

I was about to suggest, on the contrary, that such an original twist might actually have a positive impact on her shrinking circulation, although I wouldn't have put it so plain-spokenly, when she herself changed tack.

'What,' she asked, 'are we two going to do about this one?'

'This what?'

'This murder, of course. Slavorigin's.'

'Why should we be expected to do anything about it,' I replied, 'except all go home as soon as we're authorised to?'

'Great Scott Moncrieff!' she exclaimed (to my flattered amusement). 'Here we are, two ace criminologists, practically witnesses to one of the most sensational crimes of the century, and what you propose is that we slink away from it with our tails between our legs. Don't you share my sense of moral obligation? Ah me, if only Eustace were here . . .'

'Eustace', I knew, could mean no other than her lugubrious, long-suffering partner-in-detection in *The Act of Roger Murgatroyd* and *A Mysterious Affair of Style*, and I took exception, and told her so, to being unfavourably compared to one of my own fictional creations, especially as, with his unerring flair for barking up a whole forest of wrong trees,* if he was present in the books at all, it was solely to serve as her hapless stooge.

'But you haven't understood anything!' she thundered, causing a passing cyclist, a faunlet with the face of a Crivelli angel, a momentary wobble. 'It's precisely because he was a plodder that Eustace and I formed so effective a team. Good cop, bad cop, as they say in the pictures. "Good" and "bad",

---

* Memo to self: *The Forest of Wrong Trees*, the perfect title for a Chestertonian or Borgesian thriller.

though, in the sense of "competent" and "incompetent". Without Watson Holmes would have been nothing. He bounced his own good ideas off on Watson's poor ones. Ditto me and Eustace.'

'Is that what you're suggesting? That I become your Watson?'

'Gilbert, a man has just been murdered. In my vicinity, surprise surprise. For you, I realise, this is a new and novel experience, but for me it already feels, as it must have done for Holmes and the rest, like another day, another corpse. And yet . . . Slavorigin's eminence apart, as well as the kudos I could expect to receive if I were responsible for apprehending his killer – it would do wonders for my back-list – I must also point out that it's a crime possessed of all sorts of bizarre and even unique features and that it would be extremely contrary of me, as contrary as Poirot opting to quit Cairo on the very day one of his co-expats is found stabbed in the shadow of the Sphinx, not to want to poke and probe at it in the hope of outwitting dear clueless old Inspector Plodder – or Plödder – of the Swiss Police.'

'But surely there isn't any mystery as to who did it?'

'Oh really?'

'We're all aware that Slavorigin's life was under threat from some nitwitted survivalist sects whose members, even if we leave aside their hatred of everything he stood for, must have entertained the odd fantasy about how much comfier Armageddon would be if cushioned by a buried stash of a hundred million dollars. It's evident that one of these loonies pursued Slavorigin here to Meiringen and shot him through the heart. A bow and arrow, after all, the survivalist's favourite choice of weapon.'

'Maybe, maybe. Except that your theory, which is all it is, begs a few questions.'

'For instance?'

'Well, one, how would such a loony, as you call him – or her – know that Gustav Slavorigin was due to make an appearance in Meiringen at all?' I was about to parry that question with its logical answer when she held her splayed right hand up to my face, all but blotting out her own, to advise me of the fact that she had not yet completed what she wished to say. It was a tic I thought I had invented for her, but perhaps I had half-consciously recalled her behaving so at Carmen's little supper. She continued:

'Since he was the Festival's Mystery Guest, after all, there was no indication of his identity in the programme. Then two, is it probable that a rabid rightwing fanatic from some one-horse burg in Texas or Kansas or Oklahoma, armed with a great big bow-and-arrow and probably even sporting a coonskin hat, could pass unremarked by any of us, including Slavorigin's minders, in a town as small as Meiringen? Three, how did he – or, I repeat, she – succeed in luring Slavorigin unaccompanied into the Museum? And four, and last for now, who's to say your so-called loony isn't actually one of the Festival's official guests?'

That final question threw me, being the only one I hadn't expected. Yet, even if I was by no means convinced I could knock down all four of her objections one after the other, I decided to take up the challenge.

'In the first place, Evie, Slavorigin's presence here was one of those secrets that could never be held secret for long. This Festival of ours, you'd agree, is a pretty amateurish affair – also the very first of its kind – and the last too, I fancy, after such a hoohah – and you don't suppose, no, let me continue, you've had your say, you don't suppose that, when they all heard to their stupefaction, if I'm not mistaken, that Slavorigin had actually accepted their ludicrously quixotic invitation, all those sweet, bungling young people who hand me your gin-and-tonic and you my whisky-on-the-rocks, you really don't suppose that, even if sworn to silence on pain of the rack, they would have been capable of keeping so enthralling a piece of news to themselves? A word here, a word there, and it would have been all over the blogosphere.

'Two, rabid rightwingers they may be, but I really do think that these bounty-hunters – and what a bounty! – would be savvy enough to disguise themselves before setting off on the great crusade. In fact, considering the average American's ignorance of how we Europeans live, like something out of an episode of *The Simpsons*, I would guess, the kind of stranger I'd tend to look at twice is one wearing a Tyrolean hat and lederhosen instead of one in a Davy Crockett cap and leather britches.

'Three, we have absolutely no cause to assume that our murderer needed to "lure" Slavorigin at all. We've all had to pay a dutiful visit to the Museum, but he arrived too late to join us. What could be more natural than for him to take a solitary stroll there, a matter of a few hundred yards from the Hilton, and also to be surreptitiously tailed?' It was now my turn to ward off an impending interruption with a raised hand. 'Yes, yes, I know what you're going to say. His body-guards. Thomson and Thompson, as I call them. Why didn't they insist on accompanying him? That *is* queer. Except that Slavorigin is, was, a spoilt brat, accustomed to getting his way in everything, and I wouldn't put it past him to have wanted to shake off his twin shadows for a blissful half-hour or so on his own. After all, he must have said to himself, what could possibly happen to him in a sleepy hamlet like Meiringen?

'As for your hunch – which is all it is, if I may take the liberty of quoting you – that one of the Festival's guests could have been responsible, the problem as I see it is crucially one of motive. The motive of, let's say, an *ideological* murderer positively screams out at us whereas, as far as our co-*festivaliers* are concerned, I have to admit to not having heard so much as a whisper.

'Finally, let me raise an issue that you appear to have over-looked.'

'Oh yes?' she said, ever ready to bristle at the faintest hint of criticism.

'What's today's date?'

'The twelfth of September.'

'Right. Which means that yesterday was the eleventh.'

'I'm quite aware of that, Gilbert. How could I not be after all that's happened here?'

'Ah yes, but do you know – or do you remember – Gustav Slavorigin's birthdate?'

'Course I don't. I met the man for the first time two days ago, and in the Festival's booklet there was obviously no mini-bio of its Mystery Guest.'

'Well, I do. He was born, wait for it, on July 4.'

'Ah . . .'

'Born on the Fourth of July, died September 11, exactly ten years to the day after the attack on the World Trade Center. Added to which, this is the year 2011. 2 equals the Twin Towers of 1 + 1 and 20 minus 11 equals 9. The numbers, Evie, the symbolism! For Hermann Hunt's henchmen it would have been what Düttmann calls the "clincher". Don't forget, these are neanderthals who claim to detect a daffy significance in the fact that Manhattan Island was discovered on September 11, 1609, by Henry Hudson, whose name has eleven letters, that the first Tower collapsed at 10.28am and 1 + 0 + 2 + 8 = 11, that 119, 9/11 in reverse, is the area code for both Iraq and Iran (I and I) and 1 + 1 + 9 = 11, that the first of the two attacking planes was American Airlines Flight 11, number 1-800-245-0999 and 1 + 8 + 0 + 0 + 2 + 4 + 5 + 0 + 9 + 9 + 9 equals 47, which two numbers combined also equal 11, that, standing side by side, the Twin Towers themselves resembled the number 11, that Hermann Hunt's initials, like Henry Hudson's, are HH, twin sets of Twin Towers – and I can assure you there's a lot more gibberish out there where that came from.* If Slavorigin was to be murdered, yesterday was the day it had to be done. I rest my case.'

'Well, Gilbert,' Evie opined – said, goddamn it, said! – after a moment of reflection, 'I can see that, despite your professed indifference to this crime, you have after all given it some thought. And I'm prepared to endorse your objections one, two and three. Yes, quite so, a Festival of this type would have been so leaky from the start that a lot of outsiders were bound to have had advance knowledge of Slavorigin's attendance. And, yes, my caricature of a typical crazed crusader was crass in the extreme. And, yes again, although I'd very much like to have been the proverbial fly on the proverbial wall when they endeavoured to justify their negligence to the authorities, I can well imagine how easily those two brawny pin-heads, Thomson and Thompson, could have been outfoxed by somebody whose mind was set on it.

---

* A trick which everyone missed, however, was the existence of a 1973 film, an anarcho-Utopian fantasy by the French director Jacques Doillon, in which an interpolated four-minute sequence by Alain Resnais depicted a number of ruined Wall Street financiers leaping out of their skyscraping office windows. The film, interestingly, was called *L'An 01*, or *The Year 01*.

'Furthermore, for your information, I had not at all over-looked the numerological symbolism of yesterday's date. Good grief, Gilbert, even without the extra coincidence of Slavorigin having been born on America's national holiday it was staring us all in the face. What isn't staring us in the face, though, is how it undermines my theory that the murderer might have been one of the official invitees, two of whom, let me recall the fact to your attention, are Americans them-selves. But any one of them might have been what you've just described as an ideological killer. More than once I've heard you make disobliging comments about this Festival. Has it never struck you as odd that it managed none the less to attract a not altogether undistinguished guest-list?'

'Yes,' I replied thoughtfully, 'I confess it has rather. Yet writers, you know, will go anywhere if offered a freebie. Four days in the Swiss Alps, all expenses paid, and only a lecture to deliver for one's supper. I can see how that might appeal.'

'To Meredith van Demarest, who flew here all the way from California?'

'Ah, but you're forgetting that she also has plans to call on Agota Kristof in Zurich and pay homage to Nabokov in Montreux or wherever it is his remains are buried. She almost certainly regarded the Sherlock Holmes Festival as no more than a handy means for her to make the trip gratis. Anyway, what possible motive could she have?'

'What motive? You surprise me. Putting to one side the ideological motive you mention above [above?], let me draw your mind back to the revelation that she and Slavorigin had, if only for a single night, been an item.'

'Which revelation means for you that she must have murdered him?'

'Don't be silly, please. I merely register the fact that they knew each other better than she was initially prepared to let on, a fact she may have had her own good reason for withholding from us.'

'Perhaps so, yet I still can't help thinking you're pointlessly looking for any motive other than the glaringly obvious one. Remember Occam's Razor. Don't postulate the existence of an entity if you are able to get by without it. In other words, where there are several conceivable solutions to a problem, it makes sense, and it saves time, to opt for the simplest one, for nature never needlessly complicates.'

'Pshaw!' she exclaimed.

'Evie,' I said, smiling, 'no one in the real world actually says "Pshaw!".'

'I do,' she answered doughtily. 'As for Occam's Razor, we're not dealing with nature but with human nature, of which the need to needlessly complicate has been, since the dawn of time, one of the defining characteristics. And since you've just quoted Occam to me, let me now quote my dear friend Gilbert to you.'

I should explain. This Gilbert was not me but G(ilbert) K(eith) Chesterton. In *The Act of Roger Murgatroyd*, set as it was in some unspecified year of the nineteen-thirties, I had

Evie, as a fictional member of the Detection Club, allude to one of its genuine members, Chesterton, as Gilbert or, more familiarly, as 'my dear friend Gilbert'. How tiresome but typical of her that she should continue to perpetuate a now totally anachronistic affectation in order to aggrandise her own lonely and uneventful existence. It reminded me of another woman's delusions of grandeur, a woman whose identity I was at first unable to pin down. Then it came to me: Margaret Thatcher's references to Churchill, a statesman she couldn't possibly have met, as 'dear Winston'. Rewind the tape.

'And since you've just quoted Occam to me, let me now quote my dear friend Gilbert to you.'

'Go ahead,' I said wearily.

'"Where does a wise man hide a leaf? In the forest."'

'I'm sorry, Evie, I'm not with you.'

'There's a price on Slavorigin's head, an astronomical price which has tempted who knows how many hit men – and, quite possibly, the odd hit woman. That's the forest. Meredith van Demarest has, let's say, her own private and personal motive for doing away with him. That's the leaf. Naturally, whoever does succeed in murdering him, everybody's initial assumption is that it must have been one of Hermann Hunt's bounty hunters. Don't you see? What could be more cunningly Chestertonian than for her to hide the leaf of her individual motive in the forest of their collective one, this human forest which was edging ever closer to him like Birnam Wood to Dunsinane?'

'H'm. And the ideological motive?'

'Ideological motive?'

'Correct me if I'm wrong, but didn't I hear you imply that Meredith might also have had an ideological motive for doing away with Slavorigin?'

'In spite of their one torrid night of passion, Meredith loathes Slavorigin. Loathes his arrogance, his preening vanity, his sneering macho boorishness, but perhaps more than anything else loathes his visceral anti-Americanism. She may be the ungiving, unforgiving kind of feminist who wants to prohibit the teaching of Dead White Males and rename Manchester Womanchester – or Womanbreaster, ha ha! But she is, through and through, an American and, like all of her fellow citizens, whatever their ideological differences, a true and intractable patriot. And if, as a radical left-winger, she spent most of her adult life alienated from all her native land's populist rites and rituals, the shock of September 11 brought her back in a panicky rush to the soft, fleshy twin towers, as it were, of the maternal bosom, no questions asked, no apologies tendered, and to this day, and with all that's happened since, she can no longer look on America's enemies with the complicit or half-complicit eye of an old lefty. Did you, perchance, observe the brooch on the lapel of her jacket?'

'Actually, since you ask, I did. I remember it had four or five words written on it. Something about American womanhood?'

'You really must learn to be more attentive to details, Gilbert. It read: "For All The Women of America".'

'An obscure feminist clique, I dare say.'

'Possibly. But now I want you to spell out the first capital letter of each word as if it were an acronym.'

'F. A. T. W. O. A.'

'The "o" of "of" was lower-case.'

'F. A. T. W. A.' (Gasp.) 'Oh my God, fatwa!'

'Fatwa, precisely. "Simple chance!" the pedestrian reader may cry. Especially as one would hardly expect a would-be murderess barefacedly to advertise her homicidal designs. Not, to be sure, that the advertisement was so very barefaced. The lettering on that brooch was awfully hard to decipher, even for my famous gimlet eye.'

With her spoon she scooped up her cappuccino's thin chocolaty dregs and swallowed them.

'Then there's the money,' she continued, smacking her lips. 'We mustn't ever forget the money, Gilbert. One hundred million dollars. That's big change – please note, by the way, how even a fuddy-duddy like me, the me of your books, is capable of mastering modern slang. Poor dear Cora, who didn't have a truly criminal bone in her body, was prepared to take her life in her hands by blackmailing Rex Hanway.* And for what? For nothing more than a role, a secondary role, mind you, in his film. Just imagine how

---

* In *A Mysterious Affair of Style*.

some normally high-principled, law-abiding individual, someone like Meredith van Demarest, to look no further, might be tempted to murder by the prospect of dosh so unimaginably large it boggles the mind.'

'Cora Rutherford, you're forgetting,' I answered, 'was merely a character in –'

'Yes,' Evie interrupted me, 'it's true, she *was* a character, an eccentric, the kind of person who refuses to believe that society's codes and conventions ever apply to her. My point is that, where a hundred million dollars are involved, all the moral imperatives which dictate the way we conduct our private and professional lives are suspended. This Hugh Spaulding, for instance. I may be slandering him – like a lot of writers, he may be just as much of a character as Cora – but he does strike me as a man in urgent need of money.'

'Funny you should say that.'

'Why so?'

'Well, only yesterday he asked me if I would lend him some. A tidy amount it was too, considering we barely know each other.'

'How much?'

'Ten thousand pounds. Though he said he'd settle for seven.'

'Ten thousand! Blimey! Did he tell you what it was for?'

'He's being pursued by the Inland Revenue for years of unpaid back taxes. It appears he moved to London in the nineties when his books were bestsellers but never paid a penny in tax. And now that his thrillers have gone out of fashion, or else he's running out of sporting milieux to write about, the British tax authorities have caught up with him and he no longer has anything like the necessary where-withal to pay them. He also squandered his royalties a few years back on some hilarious show-business venture, *Doctor Zhivago on Ice*, I kid you not. But, please, you mustn't ever let him know I told you.'

'Mum's the word. You didn't lend it to him, I suppose?'

'What do you think? The only money I'm ready to lend, even to close friends, is money I can afford to lose, and I certainly can't afford to kiss goodbye to ten thousand pounds. There's something else, though, which may be worth mentioning. As we were all waiting to go into dinner, I saw him attempt to ingratiate himself with Slavorigin. I too may be slandering him, but it wouldn't surprise me to learn that he had tried to touch him for the same amount. Slavorigin may have been an arch-meanie, the man we loved to hate, but at least he had it to spare.'

'Interesting, very interesting. But you mentioned sporting milieux?'

'You don't know his thrillers? Each of them is set in the world of a different sport. He's apparently written scores of the things, about soccer, cricket, tennis – that's the only one I read. He used to be a decent all-rounder himself, I believe, before he took to drinking heavily.'

'Soccer, cricket, tennis . . . Archery, anyone?'

It took me a few seconds to understand what she was driving at.

'H'm, I see what you mean. Well, let me think. It's true, I'm not all that *au fait* with the Spaulding *oeuvre*. But Hugh did tell me once, when he was in his cups, that his big mistake as a writer was switching sports with each thriller instead of, like Dick Francis,[*] sticking with a single one, soccer ideally, and that he was so prolific that, in his later books, he found himself reduced to writing about motocross and curling, for God's sake, and darts and the tedious Tour de France and . . . and yes, bullseye!'

'What?'

'I said *Bullseye*! That's the title of one of his books.'

'Great Scott Moncrieff!' exclaimed Evie. 'You may be on to something there.'

'Evie,' I said tetchily, 'must you keep exclaiming "Great Scott Moncrieff!"? The joke's long since worn off.'

She looked back at me in reproachful surprise, but retained a dignified silence.

'Oh well, never mind. To return to what we were talking about, I suppose it's not wholly out of the question that Hugh possesses some small degree of skill with a bow and arrow, if that's what you've been waiting to hear me say.'

'You must say only what you know to be true and relevant.

---

[*] Author of a series of mystery novels set in the world of the Turf. When you've read one, you've read them all. Indeed, when Francis had written one, he'd written them all.

Now let's move on. Our friend Sanary. What motive are we to attribute to him, would you suggest?'

'Your guess, Evie,' I replied with a maladroitly stifled yawn, 'is as good as mine.'

'No, Gilbert, I fear that's not the case at all. I rather fancy my guess is much better than yours. You see, I already have a theory about Sanary.'

'Oh yes?'

'My theory is that it may well have been Slavorigin who tried to murder Sanary, not vice versa.'

'What!'

'You heard me.'

'Evie, be reasonable. I've indulged you to the extent of pretending, yes, pretending, that other murderers and other motives might exist for a crime which, in my opinion, is so limpid and lucid as to be in no need of such extramural explanations. Now you spring on me the theory that Sanary could have been the real victim and Slavorigin potentially the real murderer. My head's spinning!'

'Stop it spinning and listen, for this theory of mine may explain a lot. For example, it may just explain why as eminent a literary lion as Slavorigin would accept an invitation from one of the least-known literary festivals in the world. Why, I say? Perhaps because he noticed from the literature he received from Düttmann that one of his fellow guests would be Pierre Sanary, his enemy quite as much as Hermann Hunt V, a man who had already caught him out in two whopping fibs and was now threatening to add insult to injury, intellectual disgrace to social ostracism, by destroying not his life but his reputation.'

'So you think as Sanary does, that Slavorigin is a serial plagiarist, a cannibal of other writers' work? A Hannibal Lecter. A Hannibal *Lecteur*.'

'I haven't the faintest idea. But I've given a lot of thought to plagiarists, and what people fail to comprehend is that, as with theft proper, there exist several categories of the offence. [Anticipating one of Evie's 'proverbial' disgressions, I dreamt, again not for the first time, of attaching a silencer to her tongue.]

'The easiest to forgive is of course the pickpocket's petty larceny. What he steals is a noun here, an adjective there, nothing florid or conspicuous and above all no dazzlingly original similes or metaphors, which like expensive jewellery can be too easily traced. Then there are the shoplifters who, systematically combing through some rival's book, will make off with a few, but never too many, of its shorter and neater phrases. The counterfeiters are those who nick entire paragraphs, type them out on their computers and, a Thesaurus propped up on their knees, painstakingly replace every rare or rarish word with a suitable synonym. Last are the embezzlers. What they have is a word-flow problem. They know precisely what it is they want to say but they can't find the language in which to say it. Suddenly they recall that X, writing on a more or less identical topic, managed to express a similar sentiment with enviable succinctness. So, but only to get the words flowing again, you understand, they "borrow" the entire passage, intending to return it to its rightful owner when their own little local difficulty has been overcome. Except, of course, that they almost never do.'

'And Slavorigin?'

'Well, there's no way I can be sure as yet, but my instinct is that, if Sanary's energy and erudition can be trusted, and I believe they can, it's to that last category that Slavorigin belonged. And considering that he was already on a jinxy streak, it's by no means impossible that this second threat might have pushed him over the edge.'

'Might, might, might! Evie, I wish now I'd begun to count from the top the number of times you've used that handy but unreliable conditional in your exposition. None of this, clever as it is, amounts to more than pure conjecture, you know.'

'Of course I know. Just as it's pure conjecture to attribute Slavorigin's murder to the presence of some lurking loony on whom none of us have ever set eyes.'

'True. But go on. You claimed your theory would explain a lot. Surely that wasn't all of it?'

'No, it isn't. When I asked above [above??] how Slavorigin could have let himself be lured unaccompanied out of the hotel, you objected that it might not have happened that way; that, deciding on a whim to pay an impromptu visit to the Museum, he might have chosen for once to dispense with his minders' irksome vigilance. Well, but what if there was a luring after all, except that it was he, Slavorigin himself, who did it? After all, it was just as possible for him to have inveigled Sanary into meeting him at the Museum as the other way round. As for how he meant to commit the crime, I wouldn't know. But let's say a struggle ensued, Sanary eventually gained the upper hand and killed the man who had come to kill him.'

'By firing an arrow from a bow which has disappeared as mysteriously as it once materialised?'

'Ah well, Gilbert, that bow remains the unknown quantity of any theory either of us might offer the other. But please don't forget, when we discovered Slavorigin's body, it was Sanary who almost at once laid both his hands on it, something he must have been aware he was not supposed to do. Isn't it possible he wanted to make certain there would be a legitimate reason for his fingerprints being found all over the corpse?'

'True, true. Yet there's also the fact that, if it actually turns out that you're right, it would have been an open-and-shut case of self-defence. Why, then, hasn't Sanary come forward to explain himself?'

'Would you?'

'Well . . .'

'Come now, Gilbert. Let's hypothesise. Let's assume, just for the argument's sake, that you yourself are in a position where you're forced to kill Slavorigin in self-defence, not with your bare arms, not with some handy poker, not by knocking him down and inadvertently causing him to brain himself against a brass fireguard, say, but by shooting some equally handy arrow into his heart' – again the comical *Noli Me Tangere* gesture – 'yes, yes, I realise we know only where the arrow came from, not the bow, but forget that for the nonce. If you had to take so extreme a measure, seriously, would you rush back into the Kunsthalle to announce your guilt to the company which you had left just ten minutes before? Especially when everyone in that company was aware, and the police would soon have to be made aware, that you and your victim happened not to be on the friendliest of terms?'

'No . . . no, I suppose not. It would be too easy, and thus too tempting, to make a reappearance as if nothing at all were amiss. Frankly, though, as far as I'm concerned, what scuttles your argument of self-defence is the choice of weapon. When someone attempts to defend himself against an assailant, he surely seizes on the weapon nearest to hand, any weapon, even some blunt object or instrument that was never intended to be used as a weapon. On the other hand, there can be no getting away from the fact that a murder by bow-and-arrow – the bow having to be supplied by the murderer himself – is a premeditated murder. It must be. No, Evie, I'm afraid, when I listen to you theorise, my bottom starts to itch.'

I at once wanted to bite off my tongue. Why? In *A Mysterious Affair of Style*, the whodunit on which, for a number of inglorious reasons, I had shamefully failed to consult Evie, there is a scene in the Ritz Bar fairly late in the narrative where Evadne Mount's sidekick, the frequently forementioned Trubshawe, expounds his theory on the possible motive behind the murder of the stage and screen actress Cora Rutherford, Evadne's oldest and dearest friend, once young and famous, now fiftyish if she's a day and fading fast. Even if, it's implied, Evadne is secretly intrigued by the ingenuity of Trubshawe's theory, she none the less announces to him that she remains unpersuaded. When asked why, she replies to his astonishment that her bottom itches; that, if I may quote from myself, 'Whenever I read a whodunit by one of my rivals, my so-called rivals, and I encounter some device – I don't know, a motive, a clue, an alibi, whatever – a device I simply don't trust, even if I can't immediately articulate to myself why I don't trust it, I long ago noticed that my bottom started to itch. I repeat, it's infallible. If my bottom ever once steered me wrong, why, the universe would be meaningless.'

The problem was that I had invented that vulgar little idiosyncrasy for Evie's fictional self without, as I'd promised I would, obtaining her prior permission. It was, indeed, just the kind of thing to cover which a special clause had been added, at my own urging, to the contract we both signed. Now, by my unthinking confusion of the true and the false

Evadnes, except that it was precisely because I was finding it increasingly difficult to tell one apart from the other that I had committed the gaffe, I risked bringing to an abrupt end the unhoped-for conspiracy of silence which continued to surround the whole question of my repeated breaches of that contract. How, I wondered, was she liable to react?

But I could never second-guess Evie.

She threw her head back and laughed till the tears streamed down her face.

'Oh, Gilbert!' she cried. 'I would never have imagined that an itchy bottom could be contagious! For I'll let you into a secret!'

'Yes?'

'My bottom's itching too!'

'It is?'

'Yes! Which must mean that I don't even believe in my own theory, ha! ha!' She wiped away the last of the tears. 'Best move on, shall we. Autry, now, the self-styled G. Autry. What are we to make of him?'

'You tell me. Maybe you've got another theory?'

'Well . . . my initial instinct is to answer you with a categorical no. How could I have a theory about somebody so secretive, so laconic, so unforthcoming. All I know about him is what I see and, when he deigns to speak, hear. And when he does deign to speak, all I hear is yup, nope, mebbe and occasionally, if he's in a loquacious mood, mebbe not. What on earth, you might ask, have I got to work on? Yet, if you reread [*sic!*] what I've just been saying, you may actually glimpse the first little inkling of a clue to his identity.

'What, after all, do we know about Autry? Next to nothing. He's a Texan, from the accent, and he's almost pathologically determined to keep himself to himself. Now what do we know about Hermann Hunt V? He too is a Texan, and he too is almost pathologically determined to keep himself to himself.'

'What! You're suggesting that Autry and Hunt are one and the same?'

'All I'm saying is that it isn't an impossibility. The ages would seem to match up, and I've heard it rumoured that, in his youth, before he was sucked into turbo-capitalism, as I believe the beastly expression is, Hunt's ambition was to become a writer. So what if he did become a writer after all, pseudonomously? No, nothing as I can see prevents what I have just said from being true. Which doesn't, of course, automatically make it so.'

'But why, for heaven's sake? Hermann Hunt offered one hundred million dollars for the head of Gustav Slavorigin. Why on earth would he suddenly decide to become his own hit man? Where's the logic in that?'

'*Moi*, I think it highly logical. Consider. It's known – to a select few, I grant you, but what with the dizzying boundlessness of the Internet that select few probably amounts by now to several hundred thousand bloggers – it's known that Hunt will pay out a portion of his vast personal fortune to whoever succeeds in killing Slavorigin. What more water-tight alibi could he ask for? Since it's on public record that he's prepared to reward somebody else to commit the crime, and reward him handsomely, it stands to reason that he himself would be the very last person on the planet to come under suspicion.'

'Logical, perhaps, but very far-fetched.'

'Yes, I quite agree. Recall, though, what our mutual friend Philippe Françaix once had the wit to reply* when I myself taxed him on how far-fetched some abstruse French theory was that he had begun to bandy at me' – here she mimicked the crudely parodic patois I had devised for Françaix in *hommage*, affectionate *hommage*, I insist, to the Franglais of primarily Hercule Poirot, but also of that long succession of cardboard-thin, language-mangling wogs in Agatha Christie's whodunits – '"But see you, Mademoiselle, all the best ideas must be fetched from afar."'

'And the worst,' I added drily.

'Yes, of course, that's true too,' Evie answered with a sigh. But although she was audibly flagging, she hadn't yet quite said her piece. 'There is also,' she continued, 'Autry's own admission that he spent all of yesterday morning mooching about at the Falls. Schumacher took that to mean that the murderer would have been prevented from disposing of his bow. If, however, the murderer were Autry himself . . .'

She fell silent in mid-sentence, gazing around her as if

---

* Again in *A Mysterious Affair of Style*.

bored at last by all these mutually exclusive hypotheses of hers. 'Clouds gathering, I see. Don't like the look of them.'

She shivered.

'Well, Gilbert, this little chinwag of ours has been extremely useful, I think. Cleared the deadwood away, you know, always a good start. Did we miss anybody?'

'Any other potential "suspects"?' I asked, fully intending for her to hear the inverted commas I'd placed around the word.

'Uh huh.'

'Well, it was Düttmann, of course, who actually invited the victim to this accursed Festival, but my personal conviction is that he doesn't merit a moment's consideration.'

'Mine too,' said Evie.

'Which leaves only – though, as a suspect, he may be too far-fetched even for you – the tall dark stranger who tangoed last night with Slavorigin. No one knew who he was and no one has seen him since. Did you ever entertain the possibility that that rendezvous in the Museum might have been an amorous tryst?'

'An amorous tryst? At ten o'clock in the morning? I don't think so.'

'Then that, I'm afraid, is it.'

'Goody goody. Now, Gilbert dear – and don't protest, please – for at least as long as we find ourselves obliged to stay put in Meiringen, and if for no other reason than to pass the hours and perhaps the days which lie ahead of us here, I once more suggest that we two set about solving this crime. Yes, yes, I do. But separately, independently of one another, each in his or her own inimitable fashion. I also suggest, although I am not by nature a betting woman, making a wager with you if you are game enough to take me on.'

I couldn't believe what she had just said to me. Unless I was in error, it was almost *word for word* what I had had her fictional self, her alter ego, her alter Evie, propose to Trubshawe in the Ritz bar.

'I trust you're not about to say,' I answered, 'that, if you solve the mystery before I do, you will expect me to marry you?'

She laughed, quite softly for once.

'Oh no. Nothing personal, Gilbert, but neither you nor anybody else could ever take dear Eustace's place. It's been nigh on six years since his fatal heart attack, and not a day passes without my thinking of him with undiminished fondness. No, what I was about to suggest was that, if I succeed in solving the mystery before you do, then your very next book must be a new Evadne Mount whodunit.'

I had, as you may suppose, not the slightest intention of writing a new Evadne Mount whodunit, but all I replied, more out of curiosity than because I was tempted by the idea of accepting her wager, was 'And if *I* should solve the crime before you?'

'If you solve the crime first, which you won't, then I solemnly promise, Gilbert, that I will cast *you* as the presiding sleuth of *my* next book. There's a postmodern prank for you! The heroine of a whodunit makes the author of that same whodunit the hero of one of her own whodunits, ha ha! Whatever will I think of next?'

I wasn't to learn the answer to that, in any case, rhetorical question for, just as she posed it, I brusquely raised my right hand to my left ear and gave it a wiggle.

'Tsk!'

'What's the matter?' she asked.

'Oh, nothing,' I said carelessly. 'It felt as though something wet just burst against my ear.'

'Something wet?'

'You know, like a bubble. Like a little soap bubble.'

Chapter Ten

The next day proved to be not merely the strangest but the most significant of my life. I awoke late again, to the usual mild shock of a sunburst of light abruptly banishing my sleeping mask's velvety delusion of darkness. As ever I began my blurry daily existence with a satisfying albeit never quite definitive bowel movement (I knew, as sure as fate, that I would have seconds before I even descended to breakfast), and it was only when I re-emerged from the bathroom that I noticed a plain white envelope which somebody had slid under my door. I picked it up and opened it. The typed letter inside, from Düttmann, was addressed to all the guests of the Sherlock Holmes Festival. We were free to leave. The Belgian official from Interpol was confident that Slavorigin's murderer was some as yet unidentified bounty hunter, most likely an American, and thus saw no reason for any of us to be inconvenienced further. Should subsequent enquiries have to be made, the hotel had our passport numbers, home addresses and so forth. Unfortunately, it had not been possible to reserve Business Class seats on flights out of Zurich that very day, but a hired car would be stationed in front of the hotel at exactly 8.00 the next morning to take Evie, Hugh, Autry and me to the airport where we would catch the first available plane to Heathrow, arrangements having also been made for Autry to transfer to a later London–Dallas flight. (Both Meredith and Sanary planned to quit Meiringen by train, Meredith to Montreux, Sanary to Geneva.) The day ahead, ended the letter, was in consequence ours to do with as we liked, but would we please all gather in the hotel bar at seven o'clock for one last 'hopefully not so sad get-together'?

Downstairs, I plucked a complimentary *Herald Tribune* from a newspaper rack in the foyer. Not only was the murder still front-page news, as I expected it would be, I was amused to note, on the editorial page, a column on 'the Slavorigin affair', translated from *L'Espresso*, by Umberto Eco, who for some mysterious reason omitted to mention that he too had received an invitation to attend the Festival. I then walked into the breakfast room, where I spied, sitting alone, an exceptionally morose-looking Hugh and felt obliged – no, because of something I had meanwhile decided to do, I was actually glad – to join him.

It transpired that, after I myself had left the disco, Hugh had finally succeeded in cornering Slavorigin and had asked him in his turn for a handout. Apparently recovered from the débâcle in the restaurant, fatally reverting to character, the novelist had laughed in his face. When Hugh none the less reminded him of the admiration he had expressed for his own novels, Slavorigin had replied – wittily, I thought but refrained from remarking – that 'they were written in Prosak, a cross between Prozac and musak'.

'Know what the bastard said?'

'What?'

'He said I'd written thousands, hundreds of thousands, millions of words, and that the day I died, etc, etc, every single one of them would be forgotten. It would be like, professionally, I had never lived.'

'The man was a despicable bully. Both a pain and a pill. In my opinion –'

'I know, I know! The worst is,' he mumbled into his cornflakes, 'it's true.'

'What? What are you talking about?'

'No, Gilbert, it's good of you to, etc. But I know it's true. I've always known.'

I half-expected two pearly cartoon tears to dribble down his blotchy red face.

'Look, Hugh, I insist I'm in no position to lend you anything close to ten thousand pounds, and I don't fool myself that the counter-offer I'm about to make will compensate for that, but there's a cashpoint machine right here in the hotel lobby and I'd be happy to withdraw, shall we say, five hundred Swiss francs? Would that go any way to easing your situation?'

He perked up like an infant handed a plaything which

has been teasingly withheld from him. 'Jesus, Gilbert, it'd be just the ticket!' he cried. 'I've got this idea, etc, for a new thriller. Don't know yet what I'll call it, either *Murder Off-Piste* or *Death Slalom*, but I had the brainstorm staring out at those fucking Alps every day. I thought if I got a little recce in before going back to Blighty, maybe stop over in St Moritz, etc, for a few days, not the season, I know, but your – your how much did you say? Five hundred pounds?'

'Francs.'

'Five hundred francs' – a mental yet visible shrug of regret – 'yeah, that'll really do the trick. And it *is* only a loan, you know. Don't you be worrying about that. I'll pay you back just the moment I get the advance.'

'I know, I know.'

He noisily scraped the palms of his hands together, a nervous habit I'm afraid I've never been able to stomach.

'So where exactly is this cashpoint machine?' he asked, looking around him.

'Let me finish my breakfast first, Hugh,' I replied, 'if you don't mind.'

'Oh, sure, sure. Take your time. No rush.'

Once our business had been done with, I recalled that I had hoped to take advantage of the hotel's wi-fi Internet connection, whose cabin happened to be next door to the cashpoint machine. It had been empty when I withdrew Hugh's money, but we had carried on talking for a while afterwards in the foyer, and when I eventually shook free of him I cursed inwardly to note not just that the cabin was occupied but that its occupant was, of all people, Evie.

Ironically, it was because of her that I desired to go online. I own that, unsettled as well as completely mystified by that newspaper ad that Slavorigin had shown us, it was my intention, an intention of whose fundamental fatuousness I was very much aware, to Google 'Cora Rutherford' to find out whether anything else was listed but the odd tangential allusion to her as a literary character. Actually, I felt a queasy kinship with Max Beerbohm's doomed poetaster Enoch Soames who, having sold his soul, literally, in order that he be granted advance knowledge of posterity's judgment on his verse, discovers to his chagrin that the sole reference to his name in the British Library catalogue is precisely as the fictional protagonist of Beerbohm's short story.

I cooled my heels in the lobby for nearly fifteen minutes waiting in vain for Evie to re-surface, before taking the stairs back up to my room. In the hope of catching a news item on Slavorigin's murder, I started zapping the multi-channelled television set but came up empty-handed. Like the giant timepiece it is, the world was already moving on. Instead, for half-an-hour or so until a chambermaid knocked on the door and asked if she might do my room, I found myself vaguely watching an old Hollywood parody-western, *Son of Paleface*, with Bob Hope, Jane Russell and, a boyhood idol of mine, Roy Rogers, once an even more famous singing cowboy than Gene Autry, all dubbed into German.

When I returned to the lobby (it was now close to noon), Evie was still, incredibly, squatting inside the wi-fi cabin. What *was* she up to? I wondered whether I should tap on the semi-frosted glass door and make a pointing gesture at my wristwatch, but thought better of it. Still uncertain how to occupy the hours ahead of me, I caught sight of Meredith window-shopping in the lobby's glossy arcade of duty-free boutiques. She also spotted me. Yet she at once – and, I knew, deliberately – turned her face away and pretended to study a display of cashmere sweaters in the nearest window. So it was like that, was it? Perhaps, thinking only of getting out of this godforsaken dump and back to the humdrum dissatisfactions of our ordinary lives, none of us was any longer up to making the usual meaningless hotel-lobby chitchat.

I stepped outside to smoke a cigarette on the forecourt, taking the air as I polluted it, and almost tripped over Sanary's suitcase. He had managed to book himself onto the afternoon express to Geneva. A hired car was due to take him to the station via the Kunsthalle, where he meant both to thank Düttmann and advise him that he was leaving Meiringen today, not tomorrow as planned, and therefore wouldn't be attending the last-night gathering. We conversed for a few minutes about this and that until, on a whim, I decided I would pop the question I'd been aching to put to him from practically the first day.

'Tell me, Pierre,' I said, 'why is it, when you speak to Evie, you start to sound just like a Frenchman from one of her whodunits?'

I sensed him staring at me, his eyes unblinking behind his dark glasses.

'*Saperlipopette!*' he exclaimed. 'Do I? I wasn't aware.'

Just at that moment his car pulled up. We shook hands, made traditional rhubarbing noises about keeping in touch and waved to each other as he was driven off. I felt somehow left behind and lonelier than ever.

The afternoon passed as if in a dream. Rather than loiter uselessly and self-consciously about the lobby, I decided to stroll down into town, mindful all the while of the aphorism I had attributed to Sherlock Holmes in the first paragraph of 'The Giant Rat of Sumatra': 'It has long been an axiom of mine that it is when we indulge ourselves in some pursuit of pure relaxation, not when we are at our labours, tedious and repetitive though they may be, that we are most receptive to the gnawing torments of ennui.' I wandered into souvenir shops, cheese shops, a couple of bookshops (whose English-language books, apart from a prominent display of Hugh's, mine and of course Conan Doyle's, were all populist pap, what you might call McFiction, Kentucky Fried Chick-lit, lad-lit, genteel-elderly-lady-lit and, still hanging on in there, Dan Brown-lit) and even, in desperation, took a quick turn around an overwhelmingly quaint picture gallery that specialised in painted-by-number views of the same two or three Alpine vistas. I was in and out of there in a few seconds.

By five I had had it. I had run into neither Evie nor Meredith nor Autry nor Hugh, although I did see more than once as I passed and re-passed them on my directionless ramblings about the town a scruffily conspiratorial group of what I took to be foreign correspondents from the British press, boozing steadily through the afternoon at one of the tables on the same café terrace that we guests of the Festival had got into the habit of frequenting. I also noticed two uniformed Swiss sentries posted outside the taped-off Museum. But enough, I said to myself, is enough. Time to drag my sore feet back to the hotel.

Forgetting my earlier intention to Google Cora, I went straight to my room, where I discovered that a second envelope had meanwhile been slipped under my door. The letter inside, from Evie, read: 'It's 4.30. I'm going to be in the bar from now on. Join me, why don't you. It's time to compare notes.' Compare notes? She really had meant what she said, then, about each of us doing some detective work.

I found her seated in one of the bar's padded and buttoned American-style booths, a double whisky-and-soda in front of her. (So I'd got it wrong in my whodunits, in which I'd had her drinking double pink gins.) Exceptionally for me, I ordered the same, and we both waited for my drink to arrive before beginning to talk. At the far end of the darkishly lit room a blind black pianist was playing a medley of what, after a moment, I identified as Cole Porter show tunes.

'Bottoms up,' I said, raising my glass.

'Bottoms up.'

'Well now, what sort of a day have you had?' I asked her.

'Instructive,' she said, 'really most instructive. You?'

'The reverse. Whatever is the opposite of ditto,' I said, 'that's what I'd have to reply. My day has been wretched. Nothing to show for it.'

'Oh dear,' said Evie. 'Then we won't be comparing notes after all?'

'Sorry.' I sipped my whisky. 'But what are you saying? That you've made progress?'

'Progress? Gilbert, my dear, I know everything.'

'Oh really?' I said, and attempting to sound subtly sarcastic I succeeded only in sounding malevolently camp. 'Everything, you say?'

'Everything.'

'Then you know the murderer's identity?'

'I do.'

'Well, tell me, Evie,' I said, 'who did kill Slavorigin?'

At this point I expected that, like all fictional detectives, she would childishly insist on titillating the reader, building up the suspense, even declaring, as I had had her do in the corresponding scene of *The Act of Roger Murgatroyd*, that 'if I were baldly to announce who I believe did it, it would be like a maths teacher *proposing* a problem to his students, then instantly giving them the solution without in the meantime *exposing* any of the connective tissue which enabled him to arrive at that solution, connective tissue which would also enable those students of his to understand why it was the only solution possible'.

But she didn't. To my direct question she gave me a direct answer. Rewind the tape.

'Then you know the murderer's identity?'

'I do.'

'Well, tell me, Evie,' I said, 'who did kill Slavorigin?'

'You did, of course.'

'Me? Are you mad?'

For an author to be accused of murder by one of his own characters – now this was a first! Bizarrely, however, before the meaning of those four words had properly begun to sink in, they had a queer little Proustian effect on me. I was immediately reminded of a long-forgotten, although in its day long-running, television programme called *This Is Your Life*, whose guest, a celebrity supposedly invited not as the evening's victim but as just another member of the studio audience, would nevertheless find himself accosted by the show's emcee. 'X,' this emcee would say with ominous aplomb, 'this is *your* life!' The tape again.

'Well, tell me, Evie,' I said, 'who did kill Slavorigin?'

'You did, of course.'

'Me? Are you mad?'

'No,' she replied placidly, 'although I rather think you may be.'

'But, Evie,' I protested, 'what in heaven's name are you

talking about? I'm Gilbert Adair. I'm a nice man. People generally like me. Ask anybody.'

'Pooh!' she ejaculated. 'As though nice men never commit murders!'

I stared at her.

'Did you just ejaculate?'

'Certainly I did. I'm Evadne Mount. It's what I do.'

'Well,' I muttered crossly, glancing round the nearly empty bar in case somebody else had heard her, 'don't do it in public, please.'

'If I'm not mistaken, Gilbert,' she said, 'you're trying to change the subject. Aren't you interested to learn why I've just accused you of murder?'

'Oh yes. Yes, indeed. I'm actually very keen to discover how you could have arrived at such a ridiculous deduction.'

'In point of fact, it all began with a coincidence. Now, as both a writer and a reader of whodunits, I heartily dislike coincidences, which I regard as the jokes of reason and the conceits of time, and I never – well, almost never – have recourse to them myself. But yesterday, if you recall, I quoted a couple of lines of Chesterton to you – "Where does a wise man hide a leaf? In the forest" – and last night it suddenly occurred to me that my travel reading, or rereading, was precisely the volume, *The Innocence of Father Brown*, in which that quote appears. So I dug it out of my suitcase and I re-checked the reference. The story in question is "The Sign of the Broken Sword", and the relevant conversation takes place between Father Brown and Flambeau, former jewel thief turned Brown's fellow-sleuth – first name Hercule, by the way. Would you like to know how their conversation continues?'

'Why not? Anything to humour you.'

She pulled a dog-eared Penguin paperback out of her capacious handbag, withdrew a Hatchards bookmark and started to read:

'"'Where does a wise man hide a leaf? In the forest. But what does he do if there is no forest?' 'Well, well,' cried Flambeau irritably, 'what does he do?' 'He grows a forest to hide it in,' said the priest in an obscure voice. 'A fearful sin.'"'

'How very Chestertonian,' I said. 'But what has it to do with Slavorigin's death?'

'Ah well,' she replied in, I fancy, much the same obscure voice as Father Brown's, 'it so happened that the longer I speculated on the brouhaha surrounding *Out of a Clear Blue Sky* as a convincing motive for murder, by you or anybody else, the itchier my bottom got. Try as I might, I just couldn't believe it. Gilbert, some things never change. We sleep on more or less the same beds our ancestors slept on, we act on more or less the same stages our ancestors acted on and we commit murders for more or less the same reasons our ancestors committed them.

'So, having persuaded myself that the F.A.T.W.A. website represented nothing in reality but a monstrous shoal of red herrings, I ruthlessly swept aside the rubble of all my former theories and decided to do a little web-surfing myself.'

'*You?*'

'Yes, Gilbert, me. I may not look the part but I really am remarkably cyber-literate, I think they call it. This morning, at any rate, I wolfed down breakfast and, in pursuance of my hunch, ensconced myself in the hotel's wi-fi cabin. You can't know how much impatient door-tapping I had to ignore – I never knew Japanese businessmen could be so potty-mouthed! – but what I was in the process of unearthing was just too important to allow my investigation to be even momentarily interrupted.

'Oh, it wasn't easy. The whole diabolical swizz had been prepared and plotted with extraordinary cunning. Practically every loophole had been plugged. Practically, I say. That adverb, though, is the bane of every clever or, rather, clever-clever criminal. For, as I sat there, studying the screen, clicking that funny little mousy thing more or less at random, it suddenly dawned on me that, if I were to synergise the hegemonic co-terminousness of the website, all the while making sure I had accurately gauged its beaconicity – I had a few hairy moments there, I can tell you, but I was resolved to plough on at whatever the cost to my sanity – I could deploy the marginalisation lever to arrive at a degree of holistic governance enabling me to unscramble its causality and ultimately dismantle its true source and authorship.'

My head was spinning again, but I said nothing.

'Oh, Gilbert, you really wanted him dead, didn't you? '"He grows a forest to hide it in," said the priest in an obscure voice." I'm right, aren't I? Aren't I? The single leaf you wanted to hide was the murder of Gustav Slavorigin and the forest you hid it in was the Internet.

'It was *you* who created that site, Gilbert. It was y*ou* who devised those riddles for the faithful and the gullible. It was *you* who concealed your identity behind a screen – a screen in both senses of the word – of pseudonyms. It was *you*, memories of the Salman Rushdie affair gnawing away at your festering grey cells, who whipped up an incendiary cyber-climate calculated to send scores, perhaps hundreds, of pathetic psychopaths, all just waiting for the call, off on the world's grandest wild-goose chase. And it was *you*, of course, who on the same site posted an easily decipherable announcement of Slavorigin's presence at the Festival.

'It must have seemed foolproof. If – I can hear you saying to yourself – if none of these would-be hit men ever actually succeeded in murdering him, thereby doing your dirty work for you, why, then, you would simply take a lethal potshot at him yourself and let them accept the blame or the credit for the crime, depending on the point of view. Neat, Gilbert, very neat.'

'What about Hermann Hunt?' I answered her back. 'If F.A.T.W.A. were nothing but a hoax, don't you suppose he might have had something to say on the matter?'

'Oh, as for Hunt, assuming he was aware of what was

going on, as he surely would have been, he probably just sat back in his Texan castle and enjoyed the escapade. He had his own hyper-patriotic reason, after all, for wanting to see Slavorigin wiped off the face of the earth and, if whoever killed him then came calling for his reward, he might well feel inclined to write out a compensatory check for a million or two – he certainly could afford to. Hunt was the least of your problems.'

'And what in your view was the greatest of my problems?'

'The usual. Like almost all murderers you underestimated your adversary.'

'My adversary?'

'Me, Gilbert, me. Even if you sweated and strained to remove every last one of your cyber-prints from the screen, the Internet is so complex yet also, to an accomplished old hacker like me, so vulnerable you couldn't help leaving behind a stray datum or two of the kind that would lead me inexorably to you. In the future, except that you have no future, if ever again you're disposed to commit such a crime and wish to avoid being caught in the net of the Internet, remind yourself of the title of that delicious German thriller for tots, Erich Kästner's *Emil* – or, rather, *Email – and the Detectives*.'

'A stray datum or two – like what, for example?'

'Eugene, Oregon.'

'Eugene, Oregon?'

'On the page – 17, I think it is – on which you list various shadowy organisations allegedly funded by Hunt, you mention "a fraternity of Doomsday prophesiers whose mailing address was a shopping mall in Eugene, Oregon". Couldn't resist it, could you? The arch little literary reference? Such an obvious giveaway.'

'But Eugene, Oregon exists,' I said, a trifle rashly as I see now. 'I've been there. I've passed through it.'

'That's not the point. You just couldn't help showing off. Of the thousands of small towns in the American West, that was the one you felt compelled to choose. There were other clues, too, metaphors, puns, alliterations and suchlike, which all pointed to your style. Like the dream you pretended to have the night before Slavorigin's murder.'

'What? Now you claim to know what I dream about!'

'My dear, some people talk in their sleep. Typically, you'd like the reader to believe you write in yours. All I had to do was turn back to page 163. Butterflies turning into books! Books with such titles as *Pnun* and *Adair or Ardor*! What a blunder! How could you be so careless, Gilbert, when this dream after all was to have been your alibi? Reading those pages, I at once realised that, while you claimed to be asleep in your hotel room, you were in fact in the Museum firing an arrow through Slavorigin's heart.

'There's something strange about a dream,' she suddenly mused. 'It may be anything at all it cares to be, it's governed by no rules of logical or psychological verisimilitude. Yet, in a way I'm not wholly able to account for, a dream can also be *implausible*. Yours, I'm afraid, was laughably so.'

'I admit you've constructed quite a case against me,' I said fairly calmly, 'even if it's a case propped up on the wobbliest of circumstantial evidence. But, as dear old Trubshawe might have put it, haven't you overlooked something?'

'What have I overlooked? And, incidentally, I'd be greatly obliged if you would leave Eustace, God rest his soul, out of it.'

'Haven't you overlooked the fact that Slavorigin was invited to the Sherlock Holmes Festival as its Mystery Guest? That none of us was informed in advance of his attending it?'

'Well, yes, I did at first wonder at that. As I just said, I distrust coincidences. But then a foolish notion occurred to me, although not so foolish I didn't feel it worth following up. I got Düttmann on the blower. After commiserating with him about what a fiasco the Festival had turned out to be, I casually asked him how it happened that he had invited Slavorigin in the first place. Can you guess what his answer was?'

'. . .?'

'To begin with, he couldn't remember – it seems it had all taken place months ago – but with a little nudging from me it did finally come back to him. *You* again, Gilbert. It was *you* who had proposed not just the idea of a Mystery Guest but who that Mystery Guest ought to be. You made the proposal in June when you yourself were initially invited to the Festival and initially declined – only, and very belatedly, to re-accept when it was far too late for your name to feature in its literature. In June, Gilbert, four months ago! All that blether about being rung up by your agent in the train from Moreton-in-Marsh and reluctantly agreeing to attend was so much sand thrown into the reader's eyes. Ditto all those red herrings that you've so industriously strewn about. The bearded eccentric in the first-class carriage. The spooky little twins and their neglectful parents whom nobody saw but you. The no doubt totally blameless young man who danced with Slavorigin in the discotheque. Even poor Hugh. Now that *was* unpardonable of you.'

'What do you mean?' I stammered.

'This afternoon, quite by happenstance, I ran into him while we were both taking a stroll around the Falls. Believing him to be on his uppers, I actually offered to lend him two hundred pounds. Well, what an embarrassing position you put me in! He couldn't believe his ears. Protested that his latest thriller, *Ping Pong You're Dead!*, while hardly in the J. K. Rowling league, had done extremely well, thank you very much. Made him a packet of dough. Humongously huge sales in China, etc, etc. He got quite sarky with me in his lovably Oirish way, and I can't say I blame him.

'When you took Slavorigin's life, Gilbert, you not only broke the law, you not only broke the Fourth Commandment, you broke one of the cardinal rules drawn up for the Detection Club by Ronnie Knox. "The criminal must be someone mentioned in the early part of the story, but must not" – repeat, *must not* – "be anyone whose thoughts the reader has been allowed to follow." That's what I *cannot* and *will not* forgive – the systematic way you cheated on your readers. Do you still insist you're a nice man?'

'It's true,' I dreamily replied, 'I was such a weird child my parents thought I'd been adopted.'

'I'm not surprised.'

'Joke. It was a joke, Evie. But do go on. The suspense is killing me.'

'Well, the single question whose answer continued to elude me was, of course, *how* the crime had been committed. So I trotted down to the Kunsthalle with the intention of obtaining from Düttmann information about a certain somebody whose aid I was going to need in my enquiries. As it happened, though, that certain somebody was already there when I arrived.'

'You mean?'

'I mean the Belgian agent from Interpol. He was, I fear, a letdown for all of us fans of Poirot and Maigret. A big strapping ginger-haired fellow with a crushing handshake and a sergeant-major's bark, he bore as little resemblance to one as to the other. Although you might be amused, Gilbert,' she added, 'given your weakness for wordplay, to know that his name, Magrite, was actually an anagram of the latter's.

'Anyway, he was at first rather standoffish, cold if not quite rude – *correct*, I believe, is the French word for what I mean. But when he discovered who I was, he couldn't have been more charming. He knew all about my career, the cases I'd solved [?], the murderers I'd brought to justice [??], so when I asked him if I might, as a special favour, be permitted to snoop about inside the Museum, he became positively deferential. Told me how greatly he would value my contribution to what was proving to be a trickier case than he had anticipated and, right there on the spot, made out a chit, kind of a pass, for me to show to the two bobbies on guard.'

'You always did have a knack for twisting the authorities round your chubby little finger,' I twitted her. 'Remember young Calvert, Inspector Tom Calvert in *A Mysterious Affair of Style*, and how happy he always was to bend the regulations for you?'

'Naturally I remember him.' She sighed. 'What a tragedy.'

'Tragedy?'

'Didn't you read about him? About six months ago it happened, maybe nine. He was caught up in a sting – one of Scotland Yard's own stings, ironically – to entrap an international network of paedophiles who had been swapping indecent photographs over the Internet. Operation WWW.'

'World Wide Web?'

'Wee Willie Winkie. Got a custodial sentence, of course. Three years in Broadmoor. Poor, poor man. What he did was vile, to be sure, and it would have been unjust for others to have been punished and him merely reprimanded, but even so . . . Married with two children. As I say, what a tragedy. Thank God Eustace wasn't alive to hear of it. It would have been the death of him. He'd been Calvert's mentor at the Yard, you recall.'

'Now listen, Evie,' I said, forgetting for a moment the serious pickle I myself was in, 'you really must try to curb these cranky ravings of yours. They're beginning to get out of hand.'

'What *are* you talking about?' she shot back, as though I were the one hallucinating, not she. 'It made the front page of all the newspapers. Well, maybe not the – what did you call it? – the "*Guardian*"?' she said with a genteel jeer.

'And what,' I asked her dully, 'did you discover in the Museum?'

'Well, Gilbert, I took my time. I was prepared to worry the stuffing out of that room. I poked my nose into everything – empty desk drawers, framed snapshots, pipes and pipe-rack, Conan Doyle's bust, the cryptogram – everything except the blood-stained arrow itself, which had been removed, I suppose, to be forensically examined for fingerprints. Not that they're going to find any – even you were canny enough to avoid making so elementary a blooper. I knew that, while you pretended to be snoring your head off in your room, you were actually keeping an early-morning rendezvous with Slavorigin at the Museum. I also knew that, once there, you shot him through the heart, at point-blank range – if I can use that expression for so primitive a weapon – with a bow-and-arrow. The arrow was already at your disposal, just waiting to be fired. But where had the bow come from?

'It was while I was pondering that conundrum that I chanced to pick up the copy of *His Last Bow* that lay on a little semi-circular wall-table. *His Last Bow* – now that seemed to me a curious coincidence. Then I noticed, next to it on the same table, Holmes's violin, its bow laid diagonally on top of it. Another bow. Even curiouser. But, curiousest of all, I said to myself, was the fact that it was, so to speak, the wrong way round, as though in a looking-glass world or a parallel universe. In music-making, after all, the bow is a pendant to the violin and, in archery, the arrow is a pendant to the bow.

'It was naughty of me, I know, but I picked up that violin – I took lots of music lessons when I was just a gal – and began to play one of my old never-to-be-forgotten party-pieces, Cyril Scott's *Lullaby*. (Rhymes with alibi, Gilbert!) Well, talk of running a jagged fingernail down a blackboard. I am but an amateur, and a very rusty one at that, and I'm also aware that the difference between a wrong note on a piano, say, and a wrong note on a violin is that the former, wrong though it may be, is none the less, unlike the latter, a real note, but even at my pretty dismal worst I had never produced such an unholy screech. So I inspected the violin – and do you know what I found?'

'What?'

'I found that one of its strings had snapped in two. And I suddenly realised that I had also found the very last piece of the jigsaw puzzle. *You* fired that arrow, Gilbert – you fired it *not from a bow but from a violin.* From Sherlock Holmes's own violin.'

'Oh really,' I cried helplessly, 'what utter nonsense you do speak! I doubt it's even possible to fire an arrow from a violin.'

'My dear,' she said gravely, 'decades of experience as both a writer and reader have taught me that in a whodunit anything, absolutely anything, is possible.'

There followed a brief pause. The blind pianist had updated his repertoire to Rodgers and Hammerstein. It felt so hot in the bar I could hardly breathe. I finally said to Evie:

'It's awfully stuffy in here. What say we take a walk before the others arrive for what sounds like a rather cheerless get-together?'

After another pause she agreed.

Epilogue

Everything converges at last. In silence Evie and I walked through the lovely, dark, deep woods like Eva Marie Saint and Cary Grant in *North by Northwest*. Suddenly, when we emerged into open ground, she came to a halt. Glancing in my direction, she took a few timid steps forward and peered over our path's missing edge; then at once, and more nimbly than I might have expected, considering her age and weight, she nipped back in again. At the same time, we both became aware of a low, distant roar drowning out the beats of our two thumping hearts, the roar of what, at the climax to 'The Final Problem', Conan Doyle describes as 'a tremendous abyss, from which the spray rolls up like the smoke from a burning house'.

'Why, it's the Falls,' Evie croaked. 'We're directly above the Reichenbach Falls.'

'Naturally we are,' I replied. 'Where did you think we were?'

'Yes, but – but – I don't understand.'

'What is it you don't understand?'

Blinking, she looked around her.

'Where's the souvenir shop I visited this afternoon? The funny little funicular? Where, to the point, are the railings? Shouldn't there be railings here?'

'Oh,' said I, 'haven't you got it? We're some distance away from all the props of so-called "civilisation". Think of one of those tricks of perspective which vulgarising mathematicians have such a fondness for. The eye is so fixated on the sheer drop of the Falls it tends not to register that they're also several hundred yards wide.'

'Uh huh . . .' she mumbled pensively – stop it! – while continuing to back off.

Thus far things had gone my way more smoothly than I had dared hope. No one had observed our quitting the hotel together; nor, along the mountain path, had we passed any rustic busybody who could have borne subsequent witness to our having been out in each other's company. To cap it all, the moon had begun to rise on schedule. Yet I was still very nervous. I badly needed a cigarette – 'the only new pleasure modern man has invented in eighteen hundred years,' wrote the French pornographer and *belle-lettriste* Pierre Louÿs – and to hell with the alliterative linkage of tobacco and taboo. I had stopped smoking, it's true, but I remained jammed at the fragile phase when I made certain I always had a full pack, plus a functioning lighter, somewhere about my person. So from my jacket pocket I drew out my new pack of Dunhills, poked a cigarette between my lips and held the lighter up to them. Except that it wasn't the lighter at all. To my great mortification, it was a tube of Polo Mints, of almost identical shape and size, which I kept in the same pocket, kept there, ironically, I guess the word has to be, for one of those crises when I just *had* to have a cigarette and then had to disguise the fact that I'd had one.

While Evie muffled a guffaw, I pulled the real lighter out and shakily lit my cigarette at last.

'May I have one?' she said.

'You don't smoke.'

'Are you asking me or telling me?'

'If you put it like that, then I suppose I'm asking you.'

'Who says I don't smoke?'

'Well . . .'

'I'll tell you who. You.'

'Me?'

'Yes, you. In those two whodunits of yours. It's something you made up about me without consulting me first. Like a lot else.'

'What are you saying? You're actually a forty-a-day addict?'

'No,' she answered wearily, 'but I do enjoy an occasional ciggie. Are you going to offer me one or not?'

'Certainly I am,' I replied. 'I'm afraid, though, I can't oblige with Players or Senior Service.'

'Dunhills were also smoked in the thirties, if that's the point you're making.'

'How would you know? You weren't even born then.'

'I looked it up on Wikipedia. When I was researching one of my books.'

I held out the blood-red pack and lit up her cigarette. And, I have to say, unlike the Evadne Mount of my whodunits, she did appear to be at ease with it, horsily exhaling the first intake of smoke through her leathery nostrils before, like an old hand, giving its glowing tip a brief inspection.

'This, I assume,' she said, 'is the condemned woman's last cigarette.'

'What's that supposed to mean?'

'Come now, let's not play games with one another. Why else would you bring me here if not to try and kill me? Just like Conan Doyle. The jealous author rids himself of a character who has started to upstage him by hurling him – or, in my case, her – over the Reichenbach Falls.'

'Pah! You aren't nearly as famous as Sherlock Holmes.'

'And just whose fault is that, Gilbert?'

I was beginning to have a real problem containing my detestation of her.

'But it *is* why you brought me here, isn't it?' she went on, unperturbed. 'To try and kill me?'

'You keep saying "try". Why? As even you must realise, in this lonely colonnade of trees there's nothing – nothing and no one – to prevent me from succeeding.'

'I might be armed.'

'I know you're not.'

'How so?'

'You wouldn't have got through security at Heathrow with a pair of nail-clippers, let alone a pearl-handed pistol, and you've certainly had no opportunity of obtaining a gun in Meiringen. Switzerland isn't some banana republic of despots and sexpots, you know, where a moustachioed moocher in a soiled white suit will happily exchange a second-hand revolver for a few greasy greenbacks.'

She ejaculated again.

'Despots and sexpots! Greasy greenbacks! God, that's just so typical of you! There's not a single reader out there who needs to be told that Switzerland isn't a banana republic. But you – you don't think twice about breaking the rhythm of your narrative if it means taking time off to admire one of your own irrelevant metaphors. Who do you think you are? Vladimir Nabokov? A Scotch McNabokov? *The Nabokov of Notting Hill*? Vlad the Impostor? As dear Cora would have said, puh-lease!'

That stung. 'They weren't metaphors, they were alliterations,' was all I was able lamely to answer.

'Same difference. They stuck out like a pair of sore thumbs.'

'Stuck out like a pair of sore thumbs, did they?' I jeered at her. 'Poor Evie, no one's ever going to compliment you on the originality of *your* metaphors.'

'The point, Gilbert, is that you've always been such a narcissistic writer. Which is why you've never had the popular touch, not even when writing whodunits. No one but himself loves a narcissist, or even likes a narcissist – and, I must tell you, Jane and Joe Public know in advance that, because of your overbearing egotism, there's going to be precious little room left in your books for them.'

'Oh, the banter! The banter!' I cried, like Conrad's Kurtz.

'Yes, you're right,' she remarked with, in the circumstances, such amazing coolness I set to wondering whether she knew something I didn't. 'We're wasting time. Are you going to tell me why you murdered Slavorigin? And don't bother pretending you didn't. We've come too far along the road, and we're too close to the end of the plot, for that.'

'You who know everything,' I replied, 'why don't you tell me?'

She took a last puff on the Dunhill, then flicked the half-smoked cigarette over into the ravine with the sort of effortlessness that comes only with practice.

'Since you ask, I'm rather inclined to believe it was a *crime passionnel*. To be more precise, a long-deferred *crime passionnel*.'

'Explain.'

'Naturally,' she opined – said! said! said! – 'naturally, when I understood that you and only you could have been the murderer, I started sniffing around for a motive. I immediately ruled out money. I could observe, from the queasy way you circled each other when you were introduced, that you and Slavorigin were more than merely professional literary acquaintances. But no matter how sketchy a picture I had of your shared past – if any – I simply couldn't conceive of a relationship which would involve your gaining financially from his death. There was of course his prestige as a writer, a prestige you most certainly envied – ah, envy, Gilbert, envy! – although not enough, surely, to provoke you to murder. Which seemed to leave just one motive – sexual jealousy. You had both been at Edinburgh University and at much the same time. Notwithstanding his night at the Carlyle with Meredith, he was homosexual, which it's obvious you are as well, obvious even if you hadn't written that disgusting *Buenas Noches Buenos Aires* book. He was attractive, which you obviously aren't. And when you and he first met all those years ago, he must have been out-and-out gorgeous, which even then you could obviously never have been. *Ergo –*'

'What a witch you are!' I cried.

'So I *have* touched a sore point?'

'For pity's sake, no clichés. This isn't one of your whodunits.'

'I have, haven't I?'

She was right. It was too late to lie. Almost forgetting why we were there, although in reality not at all, I decided to tell her about Gustav and me.

Yes, it was in Edinburgh that we first met – at, of all improbable settings, an orgy.

He was sitting alone, in profile from my point of view,

curled up on the carpet, his back resting against an unoccupied divan, in uncannily the pose of Flandrin's *Jeune Homme assis au bord de la mer*. His naked arms were wrapped around his knees and his head was tilted so far forward, concealing four-fifths of his face, that his eyes were invisible to me. It wasn't even his body as such but its linear silhouette which attracted my attention, from the nape of his neck and his shiny shoulder-blades down along the perfect curve of his back.

He lazily uncurled himself and steered his gaze straight at me. He was darker than most in the heavily curtained room, with foppishly lank black hair, black eyes, brilliantly white and even teeth, and a wispy burnt bush of chest-hair. We looked into each other's faces for a moment or two, and I started to wonder if he was wordlessly inviting me to join him when he himself stood up and picked his nimble way through the snake pit between us.

Once at my side, smiling, he said a single word:

'Gustav.'

At first I wasn't sure I'd heard right and I asked him to repeat it. He did, this time I understood and answered in kind.

'Gilbert.'

I at once felt confident enough to raise the stakes.

'Shall we . . .?'

He smiled again, but shook his head too and said something that was ridiculous if also, when you think of it, magnificent.

'Not here.'

'*Not here?*'

'I'm with somebody,' he explained, turning to look over his own shoulder. Then, smiling still, he patted the two pocketless sides of his naked body.

'This is terrible. I want to give you my number, but I've got nothing to write it on. Or with.'

'Then just tell me,' I said. 'I promise I'll remember.'

He did, and I did.

'How terribly, terribly poignant,' Evie broke in, 'but could we please get to the other end of the story?'

'The other end?'

'When and why you fell out.'

Ignoring her, I continued.

Our first date took place just two days later in a pub that I had never frequented. He arrived before me, but only by literally a couple of minutes, so he insisted. And there was something wonderfully topsy-turvy to me about meeting, fully clothed – to this day, if I close my eyes, I can see his black Saint-Laurent jacket, pale grey slacks, grey-black roll-neck pullover, black untasselled loafers – about meeting a stranger, which he still was, who had been stark naked when I originally set eyes on him. So vivid in my memory was that earlier encounter that, the first thirty minutes we spent together, the spectral afterimage of his nudity had the effect of rendering his clothing all but transparent.

Evie's echoing boom again disrupted my reverie.

'What in God's name have a Saint-Laurent jacket and a pair of black loafers to do with anything? Get on, won't you!'

That night we went straight from the pub to his digs, practically without exchanging a word, and became lovers. Three days later, I moved in with him.

Oh, he was adorable! During the sixteen months of our cohabitation Gustav remained such a *boy*, what the French call a *grand gamin*, distracted by everything about him, by an interesting-looking ballpoint pen that he would insist on clicking for himself, and clicking again, and again; by a camera, any camera, anyone's camera; by a slimline pocket calculator; by a fleeting face in the crowd, even one that wasn't, for how could it be, a patch on his own.

As for his body, every single part of it – his shoulder-blades, the hollows behind his knees, the hairy, aromatic spaces between his toes – became for me an erogenous zone. There should perhaps be another word for 'we', a separate grammatical form, when it refers to two people in love. A 'singular' we?

Yes, we sometimes bickered, and not always tenderly, each of us boasting a kitty of pet tics that set the other's teeth on edge. He was driven to silent rage – silent because, for the longest time, he said nothing to me of his exasperation and it was only when I asked what was eating him that he let me have it – driven to rage, I say, by my habit, when wondering whether or not to buy a book, of pawing it in the bookshop for minutes on end before, having at last made up my mind, picking up *another* copy, an *unpawed* copy, unpawed by me, to carry off to the sales counter. I felt likewise about his habit of wedging taste-drained wads of chewing-gum on the undersides of chair castors and the paper-lined insides of kitchen-cabinet drawers; also of his forgetting, as if it were the most delightful quirk in the world, where he had parked the Mini whenever we sleepily staggered out of some club at five in the morning.

We shared our lives, I repeat, for sixteen months. Gustav was the first to graduate, in the summer of the following year, with a B.A. in English. But he hung on for several months afterwards in Edinburgh, except for an overnight stay in Sofia for the hundredth birthday of one of his two surviving great-grandfathers. Later that year, in August, we spent a squally fortnight together in blisteringly hot, madly gay Mykonos.

Then the bombshell dropped. (Cue a heavily ironic sigh of relief from Evie.) First, without a word to me – to be fair, our relationship by then *was* fast deteriorating and I already suspected him of several infidelities, although none that couldn't have been forgiven in the fullness of time – without a word to me, he packed his things and moved out. Next, I read – I read, Reader, in the *Times Literary Supplement*! – a review of his first novel, a novel about whose existence, about the very fact that he had written a novel at all, I knew nothing, nothing! (In the one conversation we had had, on the telephone, in the immediate aftermath of his departure, he let slip that he had taken three proof copies of the new novel to distribute to his wealthy Bulgarian relatives, to earn himself some moral air miles, as he put it, there being an inheritance in the offing, so he could surely have laid hands on a fourth to give to me.) I knew absolutely nothing of a 244-page work of fiction most of which he must have been writing during those sixteen months. But where? In the University Library? On the never too busy first floor of the Arts Café? In our own flat when I was asleep?

If that weren't evidence enough that this high-falutin' first novel of his, *Dark Jade* – a copy of which I had to buy for myself in Waterstones – had been deliberately written behind my back, there was also the fact that it was undisguisedly autobiographical and that the character of Robert, the hero's clingy, shabby, talentless lover, was just as undisguisedly based – rather, debased – on me. Added to which, there's not a single mention of my name, not one, in the index of *A Biography of Myself*!

'So,' said Evie, 'my hunch was right. Revenge for a sexual humiliation. *Adair or Ardor . . .*'

A faint odour of goat droppings emanated from deep in the bracken.

'No, you're wrong,' I answered. 'It wasn't sexual humiliation. A long time ago I learned how to put that kind of setback behind me. The book itself was the humiliation, the book and his having written it and published it without warning me, exposing to the world my private little squalors and meannesses, causing me to look an ass before I'd had the time to launch my own career as a writer.

'Oh, Evie,' I cried, and I could hear myself grinding my teeth, 'how often I prayed that he would die of Aids, that he would pass away alone, incontinent, disfigured, a wrinkly sleeping-bag of piss and shit! Well, it didn't happen like that – the creep was always lucky in love – at cards, too. He broke my heart and now at long last, thirty years later, I've broken his, literally. But *basta*. We've talked enough.'

'Has it ever occurred to you,' Evie went unflappably on, curse her, 'that his humiliation of you may actually have been responsible for your own literary success, such as it is?'

'What's this you're saying now?'

'That perhaps you became a writer yourself out of your need to compete with him.'

'More dollar-book Freud. I tell you, nothing, neither fore-visions nor extenuations, nothing can erode the craving for vengeance and the bliss of having at last exacted it. What joy it was actually to *watch* that arrow pierce his chest. So much more gratifying, now I think of it, than if he really had died of Aids at a stranger's hand. A stranger's cock.'

'There you go again. Can't resist it, can you, the verbal quip? Even in circumstances as extreme as these.'

'I'm glad you realise they *are* extreme,' I answered drily. 'And yes, you *are* right, Evie. I did bring you here to kill you. And it's your own advice I'm going to follow, the advice I attributed to you in *The Act of Roger Murgatroyd*. Remember? In the book's penultimate chapter I had you hold forth on how to commit a successful murder. Since you patently don't remember, let me quote you, so to speak: "If you really want to kill somebody and walk away scot-free, then just do it. Do it by pushing your victim off a cliff or else stabbing him in the back on a pitch-black night and burying the knife under a tree, any tree, any one of a thousand trees. Don't forget to wear gloves and be sure not to leave any incriminating traces of your presence behind you. Above all, eschew the fancy stuff. Keep it simple, boring and perfect. It may be all too simple, boring and perfect for us writers of mystery fiction, but it's the kind of crime whose perpetrator is likeliest to get away with it."

'Evie, I'm going to take a leaf out of your own book. My own book, I should say. I'm going to take that excellent advice of yours and eschew the fancy stuff. I'm even going to adopt the first of those two specific options you offer – pushing the victim off a cliff. The Falls are a bonus.'

'Hold it there!' she exclaimed. 'Surely you can see how wrong that would be?'

'Of course I can see it's "wrong"! I'm not an idiot.'

'That's not what I mean.'

'What, then?'

'Don't you realise you simply cannot kill a fictional character? When Conan Doyle attempted to do away with Sherlock Holmes, his readers were so incensed he was forced to bring him back to life.'

'Neat, Evie,' I said, 'very neat. As you would say. But please don't get it into those little grey cells of yours that I too may later change my mind. Unlike Sherlock Holmes, when you go over, you stay over.'

That truly was enough talk. A tremor of excitement tickling my spine, I started to advance towards her. From the look on her face, a look conventionally expressive of not much more than mild bemusement, I deduced that, despite her having voluntarily introduced the subject herself, and despite everything we had both said since, she still found it hard to credit that I was actually prepared to murder her. It was only when I had got close enough to catch a whiff of her halitosis that she took a first – if not at all panicky – backward glance as though trusting that there might even then be a way out of the situation she had got herself into. Whatever was its cause, her serenity suited me fine. Yet I really couldn't afford to give her the time to come up with a last-minute escape-route, if such existed, the more so as I wasn't about to begin grappling with her *à la* Holmes and Moriarty. If it was going to be done, it had to be done at one go.

My heartbeats drowning out the roar of the Falls, thunderous as those were, lowering my forehead like a bull squaring up to a matador, I abruptly charged at her and butted her hard between her Alpine breasts. She shrieked. She started waving her arms as if in preparation for flight. Then she fell straight back, head first, over the edge of the cliff.

I myself at once peered over. I watched her drift down, down, down, down, as if in soundless, weightless slow motion, circling about herself like an overweight ballerina on points or like the Falling Man in his heartbreakingly nonchalant drop from whichever one it was of the Twin Towers. It felt as though an eternity elapsed before she disappeared beneath the torrent.

I stood for a few minutes, breathing thickly, a stitch in my chest such as I hadn't known since my adolescence. Trembling, I drew out my pack of Dunhills. But in my haste, before I had succeeded in removing one, I caused a half-dozen more to spill out onto the grass, one after the other, like tiny white bombs from an aircraft's belly-button, as seen in so much grainy newsreel footage. That wouldn't do. What had Evie, my Evie, said? 'Be sure not to leave any incriminating traces of your presence behind you.' I hurriedly picked them up and stuffed them back any old how into the pack. Except for the last one, which I lit and inhaled so deeply I thought I would faint. Slowly, slowly, my heart stopped racing. I'd done it.

Unusually, I lit and smoked a second cigarette, if this time only halfway along. As with the first, I squashed underfoot what was left of it and popped the butt into my trouser pocket. I glanced at my watch. Seven-twenty. The whole beastly business had taken only forty minutes, twenty for the stroll from the hotel, twenty more for the deed to be done. Where would Evie's corpse eventually wash up? And when? Or would it have become so mangled on the river's bouldery bed that the only part of her to survive the fall, and the Falls, would be her shattered pince-nez, dangling bathetically from some muddy bouquet of reeds? That wasn't my concern, frankly. Wherever and whenever the old bat's body surfaced, I would be far away, probably back in Notting Hill, as surprised as the rest of the world to read of her disappearance. And if some newspaper solicited an interview with me, a not unlikely eventuality considering how our names had been conjoined by my pair of whodunits (but were they and she and I that famous?), then why not? I'll do anything to sell a book.

It was time I hastened back to the hotel and discreetly rejoined my fellow guests. Would it be politic, I wondered, if I myself were to raise the alarm – after, oh, an hour or so – by alerting the company to Evie's absence? Or should I entrust that duty to Düttmann, say, and confine myself to subtly prompting him if need be? Or else simply say nothing? Better play that one by ear.

And it was when I was just on the point of retracing my steps through the forest, but hadn't yet backed off from the Falls, that to my horror I saw a hand worming its way up over the edge of the abyss. It crept forward finger by finger like some unnameable spidery thing, but it was a hand nevertheless, an elderly person's liver-spotted hand, knuckles slimy with moss, declivities between the fingers crusted with wet gravel. Paralysed, I felt my face go grey and, if I hadn't clapped my two hands over my mouth, I would have thrown up on the spot.

Drawing support from a clump of bracken it had blindly caught hold of, the thing, the hand, was now joined by its twin. I wanted to die. I wanted to run away, back, forward, right, left, it didn't matter, just away – but I couldn't. I could only mutely look on as the two hands were followed by a head – Evie's head! It was like the climax to one of those splatter movies when, after being pummelled, garrotted, filleted, set alight and blown to invisible smithereens, the terminally mangled villain succeeds yet again in pulling himself together and running ever more amok. Her hair dishevelled, her eyes blinking convulsively behind her clouded-over pince-nez – yes, she was still wearing them! – Evie laboriously dragged her fat, sodden body onto the path and lay there for a few minutes, belly up, puffing and panting like a giant beached sea-cow. Then she slowly got to her feet and stood facing me.

I recovered at last a semblance of my voice.

'This can't be happening!' I spluttered. 'You're dead!'

'Oh no, I'm not,' she replied, extracting a sliver of wet fern from between the two most prominent of her false front teeth.

'But you must be!'

'I tell you I'm not.'

'But how could you have survived that fall? How could you not have drowned?'

She looked at me with more contempt on her face than I

have ever seen on any set of human features, then let loose a bitter, hoarse, peculiarly horrid laugh.

'Because I'm a cardboard character!' she cried. 'I'm made of cardboard – *and cardboard floats*!'

'What?!'

'How does it feel to be hoist on your own petard, Gilbert? For all your much-vaunted, much-flaunted "affection" for the genre, you've remained such an elitist that you simply cannot help patronising not just whodunits themselves but those who write them and those who read them. You used me as your protagonist, not once but twice, yet instead of taking the trouble to flesh me out, physically and psychologically, you allowed yourself to fall back, again and again, on the crudest of stereotypes. Even my so-called trademark tricorne hat you pinched from Marianne Moore! And if any critic picked up on that crudeness, why, you would airily retort that it was all part and parcel of your postmodern pastiche of Agatha Christie!

'You made yourself absolutely critic-proof, didn't you? If the writing was brilliant, it was yours; if it was bad, it was poor old Agatha's. Neat, very neat. Except that, in your case, it wasn't out of postmodern playfulness so much as laziness and sheer downright incompetence that you fabricated a character as shallow and two-dimensional as I am. You may have described me as plump, even just a few sentences ago as *fat*, but we both know that I'm as thin and flimsy as the paper I'm printed on.

'And that was also your undoing. Poetic justice, Gilbert. When I landed at the foot of the Falls, I merely bobbed along on the surface of the current like the page of a book – like this page, if you will, of this very book – until I got ensnarled in a conveniently overhanging branch. Disentangling myself, I crept and crawled and clawed my way back up the cliff. Oh, I won't deny it was frightening at times, but there wasn't a chance of its ever proving fatal. You can't drown paper. Or cardboard. Or me.'

'You're not just a witch,' I screamed at her, 'you're a bitch! A real f**king c**t! Eeyow!'

Blood started spurting from my martyred mouth. It felt as though I had just stuffed a thicket of nettles down my throat and it took me a moment to understand that what had shredded it could only have been – I repeat, this cannot be happening! – it could only have been that mouthful of asterisks! Asterisks that belonged to Evie's style, not mine!

'That'll teach you to be foul-mouthed in the presence of a lady,' she crowed at me. 'And what it also proves is that I'm now by far the stronger of us two. It's only by exploiting me as your heroine that you've enjoyed any real public success. Gilbert Adair the postmodernist? What a joke! What a farce! What you don't seem to realise, Gilbert, is that this is 2011. Postmodernism is dead, it's so last century, it's as hopelessly passé as Agatha Christie herself. Nobody gives two hoots about self-referentiality any longer, just as nobody gives two hoots, or even a single hoot, about you.

Your books are out of sight, out of sound, out of fashion and out of print, but you just won't let go, will you? You just won't give up. Even now, even in this very chapter, even with this very conceit – the author failing to kill off his own best-loved character – you're hoping to seem more postmodern than Borges or Burgess, Barth, Barthes or Barthelme. Botheration, now you've got me doing it! But it won't work, Gilbert. Nothing, I repeat, nothing will ever again work for you without me. Your need of me is a lot greater than my need of you.'

'That's not true,' I moaned, 'it's simply not true. I won't let you say what you just did. My books, my earlier books, they were all widely reviewed, well-reviewed too, very well-reviewed, sometimes out-and-out raves. *A Closed Book*, for example. *A Closed Book* was a bestseller in Germany.'

'The translator probably got more out of it than you put into it.'

'So was *The Dreamers* in Italy.'

'Yes,' she said. 'Yes, you're right, *The Dreamers* was a bestseller in Italy. But why was that, Gilbert?'

'Why? Because . . . because . . .'

'Oh dear, oh dear, oh dear. Your legendary love of words would suddenly appear to be unrequited. Well, I'll tell you why. Because Bernardo Bertolucci turned it into a film. The good reviews you received for the novel were all thanks to him. The sales likewise. It's true that when you were a film critic yourself you championed the director as *auteur* –

"autoor", as Philippe Françaix would put it. According to you, the writer existed merely to serve the director's every whim, or so you claimed, and you were probably sincere, except that, when it came to your own script, adapted from your own novel, it hurt, it smarted, that it was Bertolucci who got all the attention. Admit it.'

'I won't!' I shouted back, no longer caring how easily I could be overheard. 'You're wrong, quite, quite wrong! I was pleased to – I was pleased –'

'You're growing weaker,' said Evie, 'tragically weaker. You're beginning to stutter and stammer, and on the pages of your own book too. You know what that means, don't you? It means that your powers as a writer are waning, they're slowly, slowly ebbing away. Don't worry, though, I'm going to take you under my wing.

'That grotesque notion of yours of writing what you had the unmitigated nerve – at your Q & A, remember – to call "a work of genuine depth and ambition"? As though a thriller were a mere frippery, a piffling piece of hackwork, a trifle tossed off on a wet Sunday afternoon when one has nothing better to do! Well,' she said, grinning grimly, 'that's the first change I mean to make.'

'No . . .' I whimpered.

'What I see is a whole series of whodunits starring me. There are plenty more Agatha Christie titles you'll be able to pun on. *Evil Under the Sun*, for instance. That's just crying out to be retitled *Evie Under the Sun*. And then there's that personal favourite of mine among her books, *Why Didn't They Ask Evans?*. All you need do is give that name a tweak or two, Gilbert, and, hey presto, *Why Didn't They Ask Evadne?*. Child's play.

'Wait, I see things more clearly now. Not just starring me, *by* me. "By Gilbert Adair and Evadne Mount". That's only fair, it seems to me. Hold on, hold on. Even fairer would be "By Evadne Mount and Gilbert Adair". Ladies first, after all. Age before beauty. Now there's a compliment, Gilbert. Take it when it's offered you. Actually, the more I think about it, yes, the more I think about it, fairest of all would be "By Evadne Mount with Additional Dialogue by Gilbert Adair". Don't you agree? It's certainly how I envisage our future *modus operandi*.'

This was hideous, this was the worst yet. I had always suspected that Evie was mad. Now I knew it. Our future *modus operandi*? The prospect was unendurable. And *that*, yes, I could do something about.

While she was gearing up for yet another tirade, I quickly walked over to the edge, took a few seconds to gaze down into the Falls' azure, into that tremendous abyss 'from which the spray rolled up like the smoke from a burning house', and without uttering another word, without even addressing a swift silent prayer to my own Creator, my own Author, my own Autoor, I leapt out into space.

The very last thing I saw in this world was Evie flapping her podgy hands in the air. The very last thing I heard, just before I disappeared beneath the river's spumy surface, a rash of bubbles rushing up to fill to their brims the inviting sevenfold void of my mouth, nostrils, eyes and ears, was her cry of 'Great Scott Moncrieff!', faint and far-off but still too terrifyingly audible.

And then there was no one.